Destiny Pills
& Space Wizards

Destiny Pills
& Space Wizards

JEAN DAVIS

Copyright © 2018 Jean Davis

Interior illustrations by Mei Davis

ISBN: 978-1985732278

April 2018

TABLE OF CONTENTS

NOTE FROM THE AUTHOR

I was raised on a wide variety of horror, mystery, science fiction and fantasy. These genres stuck with me and when I began writing, steered me toward speculative fiction. I've always enjoyed pondering the what if questions. They keep me company on sleepless nights, when working in my garden, washing the dishes, and probably when I should be paying more attention to work.

This collection features short stories was published from 2010-2017. Several of the magazines and sites are sadly no longer in existence. It seemed a shame for these stories to do nothing more than gather virtual dust in retirement. With a little refreshing and some fun artwork, I offer them again in one easy to read location.

An eclectic mix of fantasy, fable, science fiction, fairy tale and paranormal await you. Dragons, mermaids, wizards, healers, and thieves, oh my!

I hope you enjoy this collection.

Sincerely,
Jean Davis

SOLITUDE

Zephros stared upward through the swirling clouds of orange and yellow gases outside his protective energy bubble. Far above him, in a ship floating in the blackness of space, his people slept, awaiting a world they could once again call their own. He bore the power to transform one for them, to give his people a new chance at life.

If only he could find success where all those before him had failed.

Closing his eyes, he stretched his hands out before him. Tingling power built in his chest and coursed through his body. The equations he'd learned from his predecessors sped behind his eyelids, computing, projecting. Incantations slipped from his lips as he constructed the burst of power that would begin the transformation of this ball of gas.

Warmth spread over his palms. The air inside the bubble grew hot. Sweat trickled down his forehead and ran alongside his nose to drip from his chin onto his jumpsuit. The thin material clung to his skin. Zephros cast his discomfort aside and cracked an eye open just far enough to catch a glimpse of the spark hovering above his hands.

The light grew brighter, steadier, as it coalesced into a brilliant white teardrop. The faint glimmer of hope he'd carried for the last twenty-three years ignited, sending his heartbeat into a frenzy.

Zephros imagined the sound of voices other than his own. Laughter. Footsteps. A smile. A loving touch. To be alone no longer.

The growing light in his hand sparkled through his tear-filled vision. Zephros drew a ragged breath and threw all his power into creating the seed of life.

His breath came in shallow gasps, the air inside the bubble so hot that it seemed to sear his lungs. Sweat glistened on his palm, reflecting the light of the seed.

The light blinked out.

The seed fell into his moist palm. No bigger than the nail of his smallest finger, the brown, burnt-looking seed just sat there.

The records left by the other seed wizards alluded to the idea that it should do something. Glow, quiver, float above his hand, anything to let him know that the spell had been successful.

"No." Maybe it wasn't quite done. Zephros squeezed his eyes shut and searched deep inside himself for even the smallest particle of power.

Empty.

He clutched the seed in his shaking fist and worked backward, repeating the process in his mind, searching for the moment of fault. He found nothing.

Zephros slumped down along the curve of the bubble, coming to rest on the transparent arc at the bottom. Staring at the seed brought him nothing but an utter sense of failure.

He pinched the brown shell. Hard, with the slightest bit of give in the thicker middle, its very existence taunted him. Had the seed wizards been given a faulty spell to work with, their mission sabotaged from the very beginning?

"Too cruel. Who would send out hundreds of thousands of people, only to doom them to endless sleep?" Zephros regarded his failure and then looked up through the swirling clouds of the gas planet, imagining the faces of the sleepers gazing down upon him. "I'm sorry."

He pressed the useless seed against the wall, loosening his hold on the membrane in that tiny space. The seed slid through the energy bubble, seeming to hover there amongst the gas clouds. Then it drifted downward, as if it had all the time in the universe.

As Zephros watched the tiny seed vanish, a hollow feeling took hold in his stomach. He'd need to rest for days before he could consider another try.

The computer had chosen this planet as a viable option. He had years to try and make a successful seed, but only a finite amount of power with which to create one. Already his bones ached, and his skin felt thinner than it had when he'd descended into the atmosphere. Twenty-some years of his life gone, spent in a few hours of effort.

With a weary command, he bade the bubble to climb back through the atmosphere and into the blackness where his sleeping people waited.

The ship's bay doors opened with the wave of his trembling hand. The bubble carried him safely inside. A heavy metallic clank broke the endless silence inside the bay as the outer doors sealed. He guided the bubble through the airlock and released it. The protective shield evaporated with a faint pop.

The empty bay greeted him. No small ships, no way to escape the duty to which he had been bound. He could only sustain the bubble for a few hours at a time, not near long enough to relocate.

As if he'd ever found anywhere else to go.

Drained, Zephros trudged through the dim, quiet corridors. He passed by the wall where the other wizards had etched their names. Aphros through Mephos, all with neat handwriting, their names straight and proud, filled three-quarters of what had once been a blank metal wall. From Nephros on, the names grew smaller, scrawled and crooked. At the bottom, mere inches from the floor where he'd had to lay in order to make a legible effort, was his name. Etched upon the day of the passing of power, moments after Yeteros had smiled down upon him and proclaimed him ready to bear the burden of being the last of the seed wizards. The old man had breathed the power into him, and then crumpled to the floor, a lifeless husk.

Zephros knelt and traced the letters. The rough edge of the etching caught his fingertip. Blood dripped into the metal groove. He pulled his hand back and pinched the wound closed.

Was it too much to ask for a healing spell? For that matter, he couldn't wake the sleeping sections of the ship, speed along its search, or restore his memory of the time before the long sleep. He couldn't do anything beyond the spells integral to his purpose—creating the energy bubble, and the seed. He'd tried, but the well of power within him refused his commands. The engineers had been quite thorough in protecting the people onboard and the goals of the ship, stripping him and his fellow wizards of everything but faint memories of their past abilities.

He'd had a name. A different name. But try as he might, Zephros could only grasp a hint of it in the vast grey spaces that permeated his distant memory. He'd spent long hours deciphering the shadows that teased him on the edge of slumber. Nebulous shapes of smiling faces. Trees against a blue sky. A child's laughter. Did he have a child? He couldn't remember. If he did, perhaps the child slept with the others, waiting, depending on him to create a home where children could run and play once again.

The only solid memory he held of the time before the long sleep was of sitting at a table with three engineers as they explained his rights and what he would lose. Their words were more impressions now than factual recollections. He remembered a sense of urgency, an imminent danger to his people. He'd been adamant that he should be included, slamming his fist on the long wooden table and declaring that he would do whatever he could to help. Had the wizards been responsible? If so, his wrongdoings were relegated to the shadows.

"Just give me the damned document so I can sign it already."

He'd flexed his fingers and the paper and pen had flown into his hand. He'd signed his name. But every time he looked down at the paper, he couldn't read it. He couldn't remember his name, why they'd left, or what had spurred him to make his sacrifice. All he knew now was that he'd woken here, hoarse and hungry with an old man looming over him, a relieved smile on his bearded face.

"Damn ship!" His voice echoed through the metal corridors as he made his way to the nearest wall-mounted med kit for a bandage.

With his finger bandaged, he slogged to the cafeteria. The lights flickered on with his arrival. The projected face on the food replicator's screen greeted him with the same inane smile she worn for the past twenty-three years.

In the few weeks they'd shared together, Yeteros

had told him what he'd learned of the wizards who had come before, including a beautiful female named Theros. Loneliness had driven Zephros to name the replicator's face within the first few weeks of being the sole living occupant on board.

Today he was too tired to smile back. "Hello, Theros."

"Hello, wizard. What will you have today?"

"I've given you a name, is it too much to ask that you remember mine? I am more than a designation."

Theros' smile didn't waver, nor did her eyes blink. "What will you have today?"

"Surprise me." The replicated food all tasted the same. The real food supply lay somewhere deep within the ship, locked away, safeguarded for the population upon their awakening.

"I am sorry, wizard. I am not familiar with that dish. Please restate your request."

Zephros rubbed his hands over his face. "Oatmeal." If the food was going to taste bland, there was no use attempting to mask it with names like 'steak' or 'ice cream'. Whispers of memory assured him that these were both sought after delicacies, but he couldn't remember tasting them in their true form.

He sat at one of the fifty empty tables, in one of the two hundred empty chairs, and shoveled the lackluster, protein and vitamin rich oatmeal into his mouth, keeping his eyes on the bowl rather than the seats that should be filled with newly-awakened people. If only he hadn't failed.

They'd all failed.

He should have known he'd be no different. Yet Zephros had harbored a hope that he would be the one to be successful. That hope fizzled and faded with each second he dwelled on the memory of the lifeless seed in his hand. Instead, he would be the one to confirm the dismal failure of the seed wizard program.

His stomach filled, Zephros dropped the empty bowl and spoon into the replicator's return basket.

"Thank you, wizard. Have a nice day."

His shoulders slumped as he left the cafeteria. Was he to blame for the seed failing or was the planet not suitable for transformation? Yeteros had attempted a seed three times before giving up on the one suitable planet the ship had located during his life. He'd grown old and feeble in his two hundred fifty-three years on board, never getting another chance. The records of the other seed wizards told similar tales.

The ship's drives had slowed in the past five hundred years, the engine's efficiency lessening with age. How long would it take to find another world if he chose to leave this one behind? All it would take was the push of one button in the wizard's wing—a button pushed by all those who had come before him. If he followed suit, he might die before the ship found another. If he stayed, he might use up his life, each attempt growing more desperate than the next until he had nothing left.

Zephros entered the wizard's wing, the one

brightly lit corridor on the entire ship. He paused to stand in the archway of the hatching room. Twenty-six pods were embedded in the wall. One for each wizard packed aboard the ship—they alone would walk the corridors while the people slept, locked away from prying wizardly eyes or interference. His gaze darted over the empty pods and then came to rest on the one at the end. His pod. There would not be a successor for him to breathe power into when he died. He would simply cease to be.

The cleaning bots would harvest his body and feed him to the replicator. At least there would be no other wizards to eat the oatmeal he would become.

Zephros sighed and left the vacant room. He entered his quarters at the end of the hall. Three rooms comprised his world. A bathroom, a bedroom, and a room with a chair, a computer terminal, and an empty ceramic pot with blue flowers painted on it. Someone had a plant in it once. He couldn't remember who. Aphros most likely. A souvenir from the world they'd left behind.

As he had for the last three weeks since the computer informed him they were approaching a suitable planet, Zephros sat at the terminal and brought up the file labeled 'Plan B'. Twenty-five other users had also requested this file. He wondered how long they had waited to look at it. Did it matter as much to them, knowing there would be other wizards to follow if they failed?

His eyes skimmed over the information he'd memorized. In the event of seed wizard failure, the ship would awaken its population to give them the opportunity to fend for themselves. The computer would continue its quest for a viable planet, but with no further wizard to rely on, the criteria would now be narrowed to a near exact match to the home they'd left behind.

If the ship had yet to find an exact match all the thousands of years of the wizard program, how many countless generations would live and die, encased in metal walls and bathed in artificial light? They would run out of real food within a generation and have to resort to the replicator.

Zephros' eyes grew heavy as defeat tore at his soul. He shut down the terminal and shuffled to bed. Behind his eyelids, Theros served up Zephros to starving, hollow-eyed children. They ordered him as ice cream and steaks. Their teeth tore at him, mashing and grinding until they swallowed him into their darkness within.

Stomach walls rumbled around him. The children were still hungry. They began to feast on each other. Their screams pierced his ears. Wet bits of flesh rained down upon him.

He woke with a cry, his jumpsuit wet and stuck to his skin. With his heart still pounding, Zephros tossed the blankets aside and walked to the bathroom. He stripped off the jumpsuit and stepped into the shower. The weak flow of cold water ran over him, washing away the starving children and their grisly meal.

After pulling a clean jumpsuit from the chute on

his bathroom wall, Zephros dressed and returned to the computer terminal.

He searched the records of his predecessors, as he had a thousand times before, studying how each had failed. His effort was no different than many others. He'd followed the instructions to the letter.

Perhaps a clue lay in what came after the failure rather than fixating on the frequency of attempts or errors in creation. He expanded his search, reading passages he'd never bothered with before.

Most had been able to create the seed. Of those, a few noted bringing the seed back on board to toss in the replicator. Others had rid themselves of it, as he had. Mephos logged, that upon his lack of success, he'd returned to the ship and craving the taste of something real, had swallowed it. His replacement had been hatched two days later and had noted no sign of Mephos.

Zephros drove his knuckles into his temples. "If Mephos was gone, how would Nephros gain his power? The chain would have been broken."

He scrolled through Nephros' first entries, those he'd made upon hatching to a vacant ship, alone and bewildered.

He'd found a plant. A seedling, sitting on the floor of the bedroom in a handful of dirt. He'd asked the replicator to make a pot and had planted the tiny seedling. And it had grown.

"Mephos, what did you do?" Zephros touched the empty pot beside the terminal. Cold and smooth, it offered no clues. He skimmed over more entries.

Months of watching new leaves unfurling and the dirt multiplying to fill the plot. And then a bud.

Nephros woke one afternoon to see a white flower in full bloom. Its scent permeated the air with sweetness. He'd run to it and breathed deep.

Zephros' heart thudded hard and heavy as he read on. A burst of power leapt from the flower to Nephros, knocking him back. Then the flower faded before his eyes, dropped from the plant and fell to the floor, shriveled and brown. Within two days, the plant yellowed, withered and then died.

The empty pot taunted him with the new knowledge of what he had to do.

Had Aphros known the true end of the spell and the cost? If he had, his lack of nerve had driven him to erase it from the records. From then on, they'd all been doomed to learn the solution for themselves or live long lives of failure.

For six days, Zephros dutifully visited Theros and ate his oatmeal. He slept for long hours without nightmares or the plaguing shadows of faint memories. On the seventh day, he felt strong enough to try the seed spell again. For an eternity of ten minutes, he stood before the button that would command the ship to leave orbit and continue its search. How many others had found the answer but lacked the courage?

Zephros turned away from the button.

He walked to the cafeteria. The lights greeted him along with Theros.

"Hello, wizard. What will you have today?"

"Nothing today, Theros. I've come to say goodbye."

"I am sorry, wizard. I am not familiar with that dish. Please restate your request."

"Take care of yourself, Theros." He patted the cold, flat screen of her cheek.

"Please restate your request."

Zephros shook his head and wandered to the airlock, stopping by the wall of names. He read them aloud, filling the corridor with echoes of the men and women who had died encased in metal walls.

He would not be one of them.

Somewhere deep in the ship lay a population waiting to wake, to live, people he no longer knew. But he hoped to know them again. Excitement and longing grew within him. He entered the airlock and conjured the energy bubble.

The bubble floated him toward the other end. He waved a hand at the bay doors to open them. Drifting down, he floated through the swirling orange and yellow gases until he came to an altitude that felt right in his stomach. The same place he'd stood before.

With his eyes closed, he again formed the equations to create the seed. His mouth formed the incantations. The power surged within him. Light and warmth spread over his palms. He opened his eyes to behold the seed. The light blinked out. Brown and burnt-looking, the seed fell into his hand. He held it up, admiring the pattern of grooves and wrinkles along its hardened surface.

Not a failure.

Zephros glanced toward the ship floating far beyond his view and wished his people prosperity and luck. He guided the bubble lower, deeper into the dense gas that the ship had analyzed as suitable for atmosphere creation.

There was no surface, nothing solid to perch his bubble upon, but rightness filled him. He stopped the bubble. The gas caressed its surface, a writhing myriad of reds, oranges, and yellows.

Zephros placed the seed of life and death on his tongue. Bitter.

He swallowed.

Warmth flowed down his throat and settled in his stomach, a curling, comforting mass of wellbeing. His full purpose realized at last.

His eyes closed as he drifted down the curve of the bubble to pool on the bottom arc. The bubble evaporated.

For the next two hundred and eleven years, Zephros grew and multiplied. He changed and spread, rolling across himself, laughing at the tickling sensation of waves lapping on his sandy back and the antics of the tiny creatures that scampered across his skin.

Every ten years, he'd felt the ship's sensors, questing, examining. Each time they went silent after only one day.

Until this time.

The ship woke. It burned him as it dropped through his skies. The pain brought tears to his eyes.

The first people took tentative steps down the long ramp that dropped from the ship. They peered about through the soft rain he'd used to soothe the burn. Two by two, they ventured out with equipment, testing and probing. Then, finding his sacrifice worthy, they spread across his surface. He laughed at their touch and revelled in their laughter.

With each breath they took, they inhaled a tiny fraction of his power, but he did not mind. A little magic in each of them assured him that his seed would continue to flourish. Zephros smiled, looking down on his people as he faded away.

THE EMPLOYER

Sam was a loyal employee, which was good, considering his boss would have fried him alive for stealing.

"Go ahead. Take something." The dragon nodded to the storage chambers at the back of the back of the massive cave. "I'm hungry, and you smell so tasty."

Sam pulled an inventory book off the shelf behind him and set it on his wooden desk. His three-legged stool creaked as he sat down. "Quit smelling me. I told you before, it makes me uneasy."

"But you smell so good, like warm blood and a beating heart. You know how long it's been since I ate a beating heart?"

"Yesterday—that little old lady who brought you

the silver necklace that had been in her family for three generations. You remember her, don't you?"

"I do." Green scales shimmered in the candlelight. "She was stringy."

"Krasis, you need to let some of your supplicants live once they make their offering. If you keep eating them, there will be no one left to bring you tribute."

"Where is that necklace?" The scales above the dragon's giant silvery orb of an eye arched.

"Room three, aisle twelve, pile two." Sam picked up his quill and pulled the stopper from the jar of ink beside the book. "You know, if I were going to steal something, I'd at least pick an item you may have forgotten."

"I don't forget anything."

Sam thought it wise to not point out that the dragon often asked him to refer to the shelves full of tattered inventory books. Instead, he found his place amidst the columns of entries and waited. He was good at waiting. 'Exceedingly patient', the elders of his village had called him when they'd chosen him for this job two years ago.

Replacing the old scribe was an important task. Keeping the dragon happy, even more so. Sam prided himself on doing his best on both counts. He tried not to think about growing old and dying without ever seeing the sunlight again. In fact, he tried not to think about much of anything beyond the tasks the dragon set before him. The elders had said that would increase his chances of success.

"Let's have a look at today's offerings." Krasis puffed out his mammoth chest and clawed at the rocky floor of the cave. His voice changed to an earthy, echoing growl. "Come forth!"

Sam shook his head. "Must you always sound so terrifying?"

"I'm a dragon. It's what we do. We also burn the countryside if we aren't happy, and we're especially fond of cooking those who don't show us the proper respect." Mirth shone in his eyes, or maybe it was hunger. They looked much the same.

Feet shuffled through the gravel in the tunnel that led to the dragon's lair. Two young men entered, lugging a wooden chest between them with a basket balanced on top. "We come to make an offering to the mighty dragon. We also come bearing supplies for your scribe."

"Set them down," Krasis said. He sniffed over the basket and picked through the contents with his long claws. "Sam, come get your things."

Like most every other basket or bundle his countrymen had sent, this one contained ink, a loaf of bread, a bar of soap, candles, fruits and nuts, strips of dried meat and a wedge of cheese. He might be stuck in a cave with a dragon for the rest of his life, but at least he hadn't been forgotten.

The men opened the chest. Krasis' eyes darted over the fist-sized stone nestled on a bed of black fabric embroidered with threads of gold.

He hissed. "What's this? A rock?"

"We're sorry, mighty dragon." The man's gaze

met Sam's and he spoke his next words very clearly. "Our coffers are empty."

The way the man looked at him made Sam uneasy. Did they know him? His memories of the village where he'd grown up were hazy. He blamed the dragon and the cool cave air for muddling his mind.

"This isn't even a jewel," Krasis roared. "Sam, come look at what your people have brought me. They bring you food, but give me a worthless rock."

Sam peered into the chest to see a polished white stone. He glanced at the men as he wondered why they'd brought such a poor gift. One of them nodded ever so slightly.

Why was he nodding? A hint of nausea squirmed in Sam's belly.

The dragon thundered, "Well?"

Sam shrugged. "How do they smell?"

"Good." Krasis bared his teeth.

The men shook. "We brought all we could. The cloth is very fine. The women of our village spent all winter weaving it."

"It's very pretty, but I like jewels and metal. Cloth rots, much like men who live past their prime." The dragon's long neck arched and snapped forward. His jaws closed around the head and shoulders of the man on the left. The man on the right ran. He took three steps before he tripped over his own feet.

Krasis swallowed the head of the first man and thundered over to the second. The villager screamed. The dragon bit him in half.

"They're so noisy," he said while chewing. "I'll have to listen to the echo of his scream for days."

Sam tried not to notice the blonde hair hanging from the corner of dragon's mouth. "Move to a smaller cave." He tucked his own blonde hair behind his ears. "It's only the second ones that are loud. You don't give the first ones a chance."

Krasis picked at something lodged between his teeth. "Perhaps I should decree that only one villager can enter at a time." He dislodged a section of the second man's jaw, recognizable by the well-trimmed beard still attached, and cracked it with a bite that made Sam shudder.

"If they come one at a time, they can't carry as much."

"True." The dragon finished off the headless men. "I smell more visitors."

Sam tugged the chest over beside his desk so he could properly log the stone when he got a chance. A dull pain started to throb behind his eyes.

A thick-set man strode into the main chamber. He carried a carved ivory chest in his steady hands and spoke with a clear, unwavering voice. "I have come to make an offering to the mighty Krasis on behalf of my village."

Sam's head hurt worse with each passing minute. He wanted nothing more than to snuff the candles and lie down on his pallet, but he had a job to do.

"Show me what you've brought," Krasis said.

The man opened the chest to reveal a black stone, polished to a high sheen, sitting on a red pillow.

"What's this? Another worthless rock?" The dragon's tail went from twitching to swishing, its scales rasping over the stone floor.

The muscles along the sides of the man's neck stood out and his jaw went tight. "It is all we have left."

Krasis hissed. "What happened to the jeweled armor, coins, gems the size of eggs, the gold and silver? What happened to craftsmanship and metalwork?"

"Look at the carved ivory, mighty dragon." The man held up the chest. "This box took many long weeks to craft for you."

"Yes, yes, very nice." The dragon swatted the chest from the man's hands. It clattered across the floor. The black stone rolled against the wall.

Sam bit his lower lip and willed the supplicant to produce something to satisfy the dragon. The man merely backed up a step.

"What are your blacksmiths and jewelers doing these days?" The dragon shifted from foot to foot, growing more agitated by the second. "I ask for tribute once a year. I give you the long winter to work on your gifts out of consideration for your need for your craftsmen during the fertile summer months. I am considerate! Yet, you insult me with these paltry offerings." Green scales expanded and contracted along the great dragon's heaving sides.

The man leveled his gaze on Sam. "Our coffers are empty." He shook his fist at the dragon and stood his ground. "You have ruined us all, you fire-breathing tyrant."

The word *empty* echoed in Sam's head. The pain grew more intense. What did the man want from him? He wanted to ask, but he wasn't allowed to speak to supplicants unless invited by Krasis. He had no wish to be eaten for sake of satisfying his curiosity.

"Our mines have gone dry. Our stores of treasure have long been depleted. Our blacksmiths and jewelers have gone to war with the rest of us."

He stalked forward. "We fight each other for the tribute you demand. Our fields are plundered. Our women and children are starving. You burn what little we have. There is nothing left!" He pulled a long, thin dagger from his sleeve and leapt at the dragon.

Krasis reared back, avoiding the blade. His head grazed the top of the cave. His sides swelled and his jaws spread wide. Fire filled the front half of the chamber like a red-hot forge.

Sam shielded his eyes with his arms and pressed himself against the wall. He stood there, trembling until the heat of the dragon's fury melted away.

Our coffers are empty. Had he imagined that both men had spoken directly to him and said the same thing? Did they blame him for their poverty or did they think he had some power over the dragon? A shudder passed through him, leaving a new-found confidence in its wake.

"How dare he bring a weapon in my home? I

should eat the rest of them without warning just to put them in their place."

Sam pulled away from the wall. "What if what he said was true?"

"It's not. I've seen their forges working. I've seen men in armor on the battlefields, beautiful armor—the kind that doesn't belong near a real war, covered in jewels and gleaming in the sunlight. I want that, not a pretty rock."

"Maybe the beautiful armor is all they have left to fight in, to protect their families from those who would destroy their fields and homes in search of treasure in your name."

Krasis' eyes narrowed to silver slits. His head lowered, snaking only inches from Sam's face. "Don't you believe a word of that nonsense. I've been out there. You haven't."

Sam knew he was very close to crossing the line from scribe to lunch. The stench of hot dragon's breath made his stomach roll. "Yes, of course."

"Retrieve his gift." Krasis backed into his favorite spot. "Then mark his village. I'll want to make sure it burns at nightfall."

Sam scampered past the charred remains of the man and the chest. The gift was still hot. He pulled off his shirt and wrapped it around the stone to protect his hands. He brought it over to his desk and set it beside the white stone. They made a matching set.

Black, white, and beauty shall be his demise, but you must be patient, Sam. We will need time. Sam clutched his head, willing the strange whispers of memory to fade.

The dragon's breath wafted over him. "Sam, are you not well?"

"I just need to sit down." His stool offered little comfort, but he managed a weak smile.

Krasis looked him over and huffed. "Not like you to have a weak stomach."

Sam shrugged, praying for the next supplicant to walk into the hall and divert the dragon's attention from himself. "Go ahead, I'll be fine."

"Come forth." Krasis shifted back on his haunches to wait.

A girl tiptoed in, her face perfect in its youth verging on womanhood. Her brown dress wisped over the gravel as she came to stand before the dragon. "I come bearing the wealth of my people."

Krasis gazed down upon her, tilting his great head this way and that. "And what is it?"

"We don't have much left." She kneaded her hands and looked to Sam. "Our coffers are empty."

The pain in Sam's head exploded. A cascade of memories flooded into his mind. The elder's instructions and the clarity of his purpose washed away the haze that had protected him while his people had prepared.

Krasis' eyes narrowed. "I've heard that a lot today. Are you all sharing your pitiful excuses outside my lair?"

"Many consider me as pretty as the finest jewel. My mother named me Ruby. Is not a living jewel better than a cold stone?"

Krasis dipped his head low and sniffed, the great intake of air stirring Ruby's long brown hair. She flinched.

The dragon jerked away. "You smell odd."

Ruby blushed. "Forgive me, mighty dragon. My mother insisted I wear her finest perfume. I told her it was too strong."

The whispers came again. *Black and white must go with beauty. This is your part, Sam.* Why couldn't the haze have dulled him just a few moments longer? Sam's throat felt thick and tears came to his eyes. He quickly blinked them away.

He cleared his throat. "Perhaps we should compare the lovely Ruby with your other gifts." Sam snatched up the black and white stones and darted to her side. "Is she not finer than a small white rock?"

Ruby held out her hand. Sam placed the stone in it.

"Perhaps," said Krasis.

"And is she not finer than a black rock?" He placed the second stone in her other hand.

Ruby swallowed hard and raised her gaze to the dragon.

Krasis' head returned to its usual position just below the ceiling. "You may share a name with a jewel, but you are neither stone nor treasure. You will lose value with each passing day and your flesh will soon lose its sparkle."

Ruby's lips trembled. "I beg you. Please accept my offering. We have nothing else to give you."

Sam took one last look at the pretty girl beside

him and backed away. Why did his job have to be so difficult? He was patient, but he wasn't heartless. He'd never had to make sure the dragon ate anyone before.

Sam prayed for the mind-numbing haze to come back, but he knew it was too late for that. He took a deep breath and turned away from Ruby and the dragon. "I don't know, Krasis. I'm not impressed. I think you should eat her."

The dragon rasped with laughter. There was a loud crack and a scream cut short. Sam didn't have to look to know Ruby was gone.

"Mark that village for burning too." Krasis' words were muffled by chewing on the girl.

Sam kept his voice steady. "I will."

He scanned the floor of the cave to make sure Ruby had kept the stones in her death grasp. He didn't see any sign of them, but they could have rolled under the dragon. He couldn't be certain.

The spells in the stones would take time to combine with the foulness inside poor Ruby. He had to be patient a while longer.

Sam went to his desk and sat there, staring at his inventory book with blurred eyes. How many other Rubys did the elders have prepared if this attempt failed? His newly cleared mind couldn't bear the thought of watching another person fall victim to the dragon's hunger.

A gurgle and a rumble came from deep within the dragon. Krasis belched. Fire sputtered over his long, sharp teeth. "I fear that last one didn't sit well with me."

"Perhaps you caught what was ailing me earlier. I feel much better now. Get some rest and you will too."

The dragon gulped. Then he gasped. "Sam," he wheezed. "Something is wrong." He belched again. Fire filled the cave.

Sam ducked behind the desk. Flames singed his hair. The inventory books behind him burst into balls of orange and red.

"Bring me water."

Sam stood behind his charred desk. "Water will not help you, Krasis."

The dragon rolled onto his side, his legs twitching and his free wing flapping furiously. His head snaked around to face Sam. Krasis regarded him from under sagging eyelids. "What have you done?"

"My job." Sam backed away from the dragon's giant head.

"You're job is to serve me. Get me some water." Krasis thrashed around.

You must bear witness, Sam. He wanted to run, but his job was not over.

He dashed into the long, wide tunnel he'd walked two years earlier. "I don't work for you, dragon."

"You're not even going to take some treasure on your way out?"

"You just want me to come back in there so you can eat me."

"Come on, you deserve a few jewels after all your hard work."

Sam considered the caverns heaped with wealth beyond reason and shook his head. "That's for the elders to divide up."

"You'll do what I tell you!" The dragon roared.

Fire licked at the tunnel entrance. The dragon roared again. Sam shifted his position against the cold stone so he could peer into the blackened cave.

Another flash of fire lit the main chamber. Krasis' belly bulged to twice its size. Blood oozed from between the separated scales. His limbs had gone still. The fire faded, leaving Sam in darkness.

An explosion shook the walls. Something warm and wet hit Sam in the face. The elders' weapons had done their work. Krasis was no longer.

Sam followed the sloping tunnel toward warm air and sunlight, leaving even the smallest bit of treasure behind.

CHILDREN OF THE TREES

Hemina heard the breathless grunts before she saw the ground dwellers. Their thick limbs weren't made for climbing. She peered over the edge of the thick branch, catching a glimpse of their sweaty, dirt-smeared faces.

"Get back from there." Her father's long fingers wrapped around her arm.

The woven vines of the ladders creaked under the weight of so many ground dwellers. Her ears swiveled, picking up similar sounds from the surrounding trees.

Her father's round, brown eyes narrowed and he shook his head, sending the long fringe of fur along his jawline swinging to and fro. "There are so many.

29

Quick, get inside."

"Why?" Hemina's heart pounded. She'd had never seen the ground dwellers up close. "Surely the trees will protect us if we are in danger."

"Open your mind, girl. You'll hear them."

She calmed her mind and listened, the rustle of leaves becoming a whisper that tickled her ears. *Hide.*

The fine brown fur that covered her body stood on end. Ground dwellers had never desired her people. The depth of their generations-long relations had only ever reached a wary level of trading, but that happened from the ground where they used a webwork of baskets on long ropes to exchange their goods. The ground dwellers weren't slavers and they'd kept their warring ways far from her forest.

But now they were here, climbing the trees. Surely, if they'd made it up the ladders this far, they'd been invited? Nagea had charged the trees to protect her chosen people.

She backed away from the edge, the pads of her feet moving silently over the rough bark. When she reached the fissure that served as their doorway, she clutched the edge, ready to bolt into the shadows, but curiosity compelled her to stay.

On the tree beside theirs, men slowly crept upward. Sunshine snuck through the thick canopy high overhead to catch on steel bound to their backs. If they bared their weapons, would the trees attack? Her fingernails dug into the bark.

The eight ground dwellers on the next tree reached the first ledge. They spilled over the top, one after the other. The leaves went silent. Hemina sensed everyone had gone silent, waiting and watching.

The ground dwellers scrambled away from the edge, hugging the trunk of the tree. Four made their way over to the next section of ladder, continuing upward. The others spoke in their odd tongue.

"What are they saying?" she asked her father.

He cocked his head and his ears twitched. "They only want the women who are with child. The rest will die." He backed up, bumping into Hemina and driving her into their home. "Nagea save us, the prophecy the elders have whispered of is unfolding."

Screams filled the air. Hemina cowered behind her father. The trees began to whisper again. *Hide. Hide. Hide.*

The air grew thick around them as their home tree's mood changed. Branches creaked. Leaves wove closer together, blocking out the sunlight. A cloak of darkness fell upon the forest.

The ground dwellers yelled to one another. Bright specks of light burst into being. Fire. Hemina whimpered. She'd seen it on the forest floor when traders came, points of flickering light far below her. Down there, controlled with rings of stone, she'd been told fire was safe. But here, in the trees, it could be deadly.

The fissure narrowed but the tree didn't swallow them in its wooden embrace. It left enough space for Hemina to see and to get fresh air, a hole to the outside world that could have been nothing more than an opening to a bird's nest.

More screams. A thick thud echoed, keeping time with the vibrations that ran through the trunk that surrounded them.

"Axes," said her father. He dropped to his knees and pulled her down beside him. He began to pray.

Hemina's gaze flitted over the items in the room in search of a weapon. Her sewing chest, their table, their food stores, a mound of furs; none of these things would protect her from men with axes and fire. In all the years they'd traded with the ground dwellers, not one of them had ever brought a weapon. The most she had were the long bone needles that she used to weave the cloth her people made from the threads the ground dwellers brought. Cloth her people then traded for furs and goods. Goods made from the dead trees, plants, and animals. She bowed her head and joined her father in prayer. The beautiful goddess of her people would protect them.

The stink of burning wood and furs crept through the hole. Smoke tickled her nose. Hemina sneezed.

Orange light flickered outside, filling their room with nightmarish shadows that leapt from one wall to the other. Her father prayed louder and faster.

She crept to the fissure to peek outside. Two of her cousins, their bellies round with child, stood on the branch outside surrounded by six ground dwellers armed with steel. The branch trembled as if the tree were trying to shake off the offending ground dwellers. It grew so violent that the whole tree trunk shook. Wood groaned all around her. Food toppled from ledges and spilled onto the floor, bouncing and rolling underfoot. Hemina shrieked.

One of the men spun around, his gaze meeting hers. She ducked, cowering below the hole. His arm reached through, searching blindly.

"What have you done?" Her father yanked her away from the opening. He shoved her down onto the floor and piled the furs over her. Their weight bore down on her head and back. The smoke grew thicker. She peered through a gap only large enough for one eye.

Her father stood beside the opening with the sewing chest in his hands. A loud thud hit the trunk, again and again, until wood began to fly through the air. Splinters and chips sprayed from the growing opening, littering the floor with shards of Nagea's tree. A deep shudder passed through the wood.

The torch came through first, then the man holding it. Her father smashed the chest over the intruder's head. The torch fell to the floor. The man grunted and stumbled to his knees, but as her father sought another weapon, the man regained his footing. He swung the axe, catching her father in the neck. The man grabbed the torch before the fire took to the green wood of the trunk.

Her father clutched his throat, blood gushing between his fingers. His lips formed the prayer to Nagea, but his voice was silent.

Hemina squeezed her eyes shut. The trees cried

out. Fires licked at them, building into furnaces fueled by trade goods and devouring living wood with agonizing slowness and billowing smoke. Axes carved out gaping wounds in their flesh. And still, Negea didn't come. Hemina prayed harder.

A sharp pain tore through her stomach. Hemina lost her breath. She clutched her belly. Something moved within her, writhing, expanding. She screamed as her abdomen muscles ripped and her flat belly inflated to a giant orb as though she were ready to give birth at any moment.

Hemina had seen her pregnant cousins standing outside unharmed. Nagea had heard her prayers.

A hand ripped her hiding place away. The man flashed a blunt-toothed smile and stepped towards her with the torch in his hand. The axe hung from his belt. He yelled something to the men outside.

Hemina lunged for the axe. The man jumped back and two more rushed in, grabbing her. The first man pointed her toward the opening. Though she struggled against them, her captors pulled her past her father who stared up at her from the floor with empty eyes. His lips had gone still. His prayers unanswered.

Tears ran down her face. The trees cried with her, mourning the loss of so many.

Once outside, Hemina spotted her cousins on the lower ladder, making their way to the ground with an escort of armed men. Bile filled her throat. The unclean ground would taint them. They would never be allowed to return to the trees.

Embers rained down as fire took hold in the upper homes, burning the leaves above. The heavy smoke masked the horror that accompanied piercing screams and unanswered cries for mercy.

She glanced at her heavy stomach. She might be saved, but she would also be made unclean. "What have you done?" she cried to her goddess and the men who held her.

The men ignored her, merely guiding her to the downward ladder. A pressure in her head answered, but its voice wasn't feminine as she had expected.

"*It's more what you have done, sweetling.*" The low voice chuckled. "*You opened yourself up to your goddess, but sadly she was occupied elsewhere. That was a lot of trouble, I'll have you know.*"

The men pushed and poked at her until she swung her unfamiliar bulk over the edge of the branch and found the first rung with her long toes. Once she had a solid handhold on the rungs, she held on tight, refusing to move.

"Who are you?"

"*You asked for help. I answered. Do we really need to quibble about who I am?*"

The man above her scowled and yelled. When she still didn't move, he pried at her fingers. Hemina let go with one hand but only to claw at his. The man below her yanked on her feet. She kicked at him, connecting with his face. The weight of her belly pulled her off balance and her one-handed grip slipped. A bloody hand grabbed hers, forcing it back onto the rung. The scowling man yelled again, pointing downward.

"Why are you doing this?" she asked the thing within her.

It rolled again, twisting and writhing like an eel.

"*There's a prophecy among my followers. I'm to be birthed from one of you. There may be a little wiggle room for interpretation, but prophecies need to be fulfilled or people stop believing.*"

"What if I don't want to give birth to you?"

"*Let's call this a partnership, shall we? You give birth, I let you live. I'll tell you what; I'll even have them worship you.*"

The man above planted his feet on the rung where she held on. His foot ground into the bones of her fingers. Hemina yelped and moved down a rung. He kept coming, driving her downward. When they reached the home below hers, the men paused to catch their breaths but they remained at her side.

"*Come now, sweetling. You'll enjoy it. See how my men protect you? Get to the ground, and we'll both be safe.*"

"Both of us? You're not much of a god."

A sharp pain in her stomach took her breath away. Hemina doubled over, clutching her belly. The men muttered, glancing over the edge to the ground still far below.

"*Mind what you say, sweetling. I could always have them kill you the moment I'm reborn into your world.*"

The blood of her people stained the branch where she stood. "The trees will never let your men reach the ground."

"*Trees, trees, trees. That's all you people talk about, isn't it? There's much more in your world beyond the damned leaves and branches. Not that your kind has ever come down from your trees long enough to see it.*" The sharp pain again tore through her belly. "*Better move, sweetling. No time to waste.*"

The men rushed her to the ladder, three of them going down first before the one with the big feet pushed her to the edge and downward. Hemina cried out to Nagea and the trees.

"*They can't save you. Only I can.*"

The pain settled into the bottom of her stomach, building up with intense pressure. A blazing branch plummeted past her, followed by the flailing body of one of her people.

Far below, her cousins stood amidst the ferns, heads bowed and surrounded by men.

Another round of shattering pain built up within her. Hemina's lips drew tight and her hands shook as she grasped the next rung. She tried to hold it back, but a cry tore from her lips.

"*If you don't get to the ground, I'll have them kill your friends. They are not chosen as you are.*"

"They're already dead."

"*Serve me and I will allow them to live to serve you.*"

The tree shuddered, shaking the ladder and those who clung to it. It was as if the trees had given up hope of preserving her people and just wanted them all gone. Hemina opened her mind, trying to offer the trees comfort but smoke filled her lungs. A wracking round of coughs brought an end to her efforts.

The man below her yelled to those above. They

all moved faster. She had no choice but to move with them. The ground grew closer.

"I don't want to be served or worshipped. I want my father, my people, and my trees back."

"*I want to be born. Get moving.*"

"No." Hemina halted.

The feet of the man above her stomped on her fingers. He waved at her with one hand as if he could shove her downward with the gesture. The man below tugged on her feet.

A huge branch crashed down through the smoke, smashing the ladder of the tree beside them. The ladder disintegrated, sending those on it shrieking to their bone-shattering deaths on their beloved ground.

Hemina took a deep breath and closed her eyes, blocking out the frantic yelling of the surrounding men and the crackling of the burning wood above her. Her goddess might be silent, but the trees were not. She sought out her home tree, sharing the pain of another contraction with its pain of burning. Together they screamed.

The tree spoke slowly, its voice as rough as its bark. *Together. End together.*

A tremor ran down the ladder. The babbling grew to a fervent pleading. The man below her deserted his position and started downward.

An ear-piercing crack ran through the tree from top to bottom. Burning wood and leaves rained down upon them. Men cried out as embers scorched their bare skin.

"What have you done?" The god inside her rolled and tumbled.

Above her, one man lost his grip on the ladder. He flailed for a second, his feet still on the rungs. The men near him reached out, but they couldn't reach him. He flailed all the way to the ground.

The upturned faces of the men on the ground were filled with horror. Her cousins grinned. The dry leaves and branches on the forest floor burst into flames.

The men on the ground scattered.

A horrible shifting feeling passed through Hemina as her home tree lurched sideways. The presence of the tree that had been with her since birth faded as it severed its deep roots one by one.

"No, no, no!" The god pummeled her insides. *"We're not close enough to the bottom. Down, get down!"*

"I will never touch the ground."

The man above her scrambled over her, trampling her hands and body. Her shattered fingers refused to hold on any longer. Hemina let go, taking the two men passing over her with her as she fell.

The trees went silent. Men screamed, as did the god inside her.

Leaves fell all around her, reminding her of soft winds blowing through them above her bed at night. The cool rushing air comforted the burns on her arms and back.

Above her, the last of the ladders crumbled. Men flailed and fell. A deep earth-wrenching rumble filled the air. The trees toppled.

Hemina held her arms outstretched, welcoming the embrace of the trees and her goddess. A thick branch caught her in the stomach, piercing her through like the steel the men had carried. The god within her went silent and still.

She caressed the wood, its rough bark comforting her until it came to a jolting stop when the end of it dove into the ground. Her feet dangled just above the ferns.

FOUND

The first time Adam McIntire hid, he was four years old. Sick of being dragged from one store to the next, he only wanted to hide for a few minutes, just long enough to rest his feet and escape the shrill voices of the salesladies and their cheek-pinching fingers. He squeezed his eyes shut and wished himself hidden with all his might.

Deep within a clothing rack, shivers rushed over his skin. A wave of dizziness made him clutch the rack with both hands. The store got quiet like he'd put a pillow over his head. His mother called him, but she sounded so far away.

Adam opened his eyes to find the colorful rack of clothing had turned to shades of gray. His let go of the rack with one hand to touch the strange cloth and found that his skin had also turned pale gray.

"What's your name?" someone behind him asked.

He turned around, pushing clothes aside. His hair caught on a zipper. He yelped and tugged it free.

A little girl, near the same age as himself, stood in the rack with him. Even though it was a chilly fall day, she wore shorts and a t-shirt. And she was gray. Her black within black eyes stared at him. "I'm Caroline," she said.

"I'm Adam." He frowned at the sound of his voice. It was like when his mother pushed the button for the radio station that didn't come in quite right, all scratchy with static and missing parts of words. He jabbed a finger into his ear and wiggled it around. "Where's your mommy?"

"She's not here."

The finger didn't help. His voice still sounded weird. So did hers.

"Want to play?" she asked.

"No." His scalp hurt and her weird voice made his skin all prickly. He wanted his mom to find him. Adam let go of the rack and stepped out of the wall of clothing.

Caroline grabbed his hand. "I want to play."

The whole store had gone gray. Salesladies folded gray clothes and smiled at gray shoppers. Children held their mother's gray hands. A deep hum buzzed all around. He could make out bits of what the adults were saying and what sounded like a baby crying somewhere.

His mother yanked the clothes hangers apart on the racks as she came closer. A saleslady talked to her and started looking too. Soon after, a third joined them.

Caroline let go of his hand and tapped him on the shoulder. "You're it."

Tears welled in Adam's eyes, making Caroline's smiling, gray face blur. "I don't want to play. I want to go home."

His mother walked right past him. He reached out for her but his hand went right through her leg like it was pudding. She stopped for a second and looked around but then moved on to the next rack.

"Mommy!" he yelled.

Caroline scowled. "Don't be such a baby."

"I'm not."

Adam didn't want Caroline to see him cry. He darted back into the middle of the rack and squeezed his eyes shut, wishing more than anything else to be found.

Bright light penetrated his eyelids. Adam found himself once again surrounded by dark blue pants and yellow and orange shirts, some with bright floral prints and others with white stripes.

"He's here. I found him," shouted one of the salesladies.

Adam's mother raced over and plucked him from the rack. She squeezed him tight to her chest. "I swear I just looked there. Thank you."

Her heartbeat pounded in Adam's ear as he pressed himself against her silky red shirt. Her arms were shaking and her voice had turned to sobs.

"Really, thank you so much," she said to the lady.

She kissed Adam's forehead and strode out of the store with him in her arms. "Don't tell your father I lost you. We'll both be in trouble."

"I won't." Adam knew better than that.

Though part of him was afraid, he was curious about Caroline and the gray place. He didn't know what he'd done to get there, but he thought that if he could get to the gray place at home when he wanted to, maybe it wouldn't be so scary. Over the next few months, he huddled under the covers at night, asking Caroline to play, but she never came, nor did the hum or the gray. He sat in his dark closet, surrounded by clothes, waiting. But she didn't come.

It wasn't until his father came home drunk one night, yelling, and banging things around, that Adam grabbed his blanket, hid under his bed, squeezed his eyes shut, that heard the hum of the gray place.

Caroline lay across from him. She smiled. "I've missed you. Can you play now?"

The hum drowned out his father's yelling and, if he concentrated on Caroline's voice, his mother's high-pitched voice too. His father couldn't touch him. Here, in the gray place, he was free to do whatever he wanted. Adam smiled back. "Yes."

They spent the night jumping on his bed, playing with his toys, and telling stories. When finally Adam's eyes wanted to close, he wished the gray place away.

"Not like that." Caroline laughed. "I'll only tell

you the way if you promise to come back and play with me again."

"I promise."

"Good." She took his hand and tugged him down to the floor. They huddled under his bed on his blanket. Caroline held his hand tight. "You promise, right?"

Adam nodded.

"You gotta be where you were when you hid and then wish to be found."

He closed his eyes and wished just like he had in the store months ago. Only this time, he wasn't crying, and he wasn't scared. He was just really tired.

The hum remained in his ears and Caroline still held his hand, but he couldn't stay awake any longer.

He woke to his mother peering under the bed, calling his name. "There you are." She pulled his blanket, sliding him out from under the bed. Sunlight beamed through his window, filling the room with a warm yellow glow. A rainbow scatter of toys littered his floor. "Why are you under there?"

Adam yawned. "You were too loud."

His mother's face turned red. "Oh. I thought you were sleeping. I didn't think…" Tears welled in her eyes. "I'm sorry, baby. Daddy's gone."

Adam considered that he was probably supposed to cry too, but he was happy Daddy was gone. It was the bruise on his mother's cheek that made tears comes to his eyes.

He had wished to be found, and she had done just that. Daddy wouldn't have ever found him. He wouldn't have even tried. Adam hugged his mother.

The next night he waited until he heard his mother's bedroom door close before sliding under his bed. He closed his eyes and hid there until he heard the hum. Caroline's static-edged giggle came seconds later.

"I knew you'd come back." She clapped her hands. "What do you want to play first?"

He picked up a car and pushed it across the floor to her. With the hum surrounding him, he could barely hear the sound of hard plastic wheels on wood—a sound that would have normally brought his mother running into his room to tell him to get back into bed and go to sleep. Even in the quiet house, they could be as loud as they wanted. Adam let out a whoop and grabbed the drum his aunt had given him. He pounded out a wild beat while Caroline danced. They spent the night building towers with wooden blocks and smashing them down with cars, feet, and pillows.

When it came morning, his mother again found him under his bed. She ruffled his hair. "You look so tired. Did you get any sleep at all?"

Adam knew better than to lie to his mother. He shook his head.

"This is a hard time for both of us, I suppose." She sighed. "How about I make you breakfast and then you take a little nap before we get this day started?"

He sat at the wooden table, chin in hands, trying to keep his eyes open while she made pancakes. "Is

Daddy coming back?"

"No." She touched the bruise on her cheek and grimaced. "Not this time." She slid a plate of steaming cakes in front of him and drizzled them with sweet syrup.

Adam gobbled them down. Feeling safe and full, he climbed into his bed and slept. However, his mother didn't let him nap long, and so when she put him to bed at the end of the day, he was far too tired to play with Caroline. The next night his mother was sad so he stayed up late, curled in her arms, watching television until he dozed off. He woke up in his bed. On the third night, there was a phone call.

From the living room, he could hear his mother screaming into the phone in the kitchen. She even said the words she'd told him never to repeat. She said them lots of times and loudly.

"You are not coming over here," she yelled. "I told you that you couldn't see him. I don't care if he's your son or not."

Adam put his hands over his ears and burrowed into the couch pillows. The sound of the phone slamming into the counter exploded through his shaking hands.

He ran into his room and closed the door. Her words had never stopped Daddy from throwing and breaking things or from hitting her or yelling at him.

Daddy was coming.

He swept his books from his bookshelf and pushed it in front of the door. He piled his heaviest toys on the shelves. Adam clutched his blanket and slid under his bed, curling into a ball. He wasn't hidden enough.

The hum of the gray place surrounded him.

Caroline squealed. "You're back! Where have you been? Didn't we have fun together?"

"Yes." He forced a shaky smile, but his lips couldn't lie either.

"What's wrong?"

The gray would hide him better than any bed could. Daddy could come and throw everything he wanted. He could even break down the door and smash the bookcase. Daddy still wouldn't find him unless he wanted to be found. He was safe here.

"Nothing. Let's play."

Adam tried to build a tower but they'd scattered so many blocks last time that he couldn't build it higher than his knees. Caroline pounded on the drum and told him to dance, but his feet didn't want to. He kept glancing at the door. She tried to play cars with him, but even though he knew the sound didn't go outside the gray, every throaty rev and rumble made him more nervous.

"Let's look at a book," he suggested.

"Sure." Caroline picked one from the scattered pile on the floor and sat down next to him.

"I can't read good," Adam said. He wished his mother would read him a story right now. To be able to sit on her lap, to hear her heartbeat as he leaned against her chest, would make him feel safe.

"That's okay. I can read." Caroline began the story of a boy lost in the woods and a talking squirrel.

The static in her voice and the clipped words kept him from drifting off into his imagination like when his mother read to him.

He wanted her to stop. He didn't want to play. He just wanted to hide. But he needed the gray for that and Caroline came with it. Adam sat and listened, but he wasn't listening to the story, he was listening for his mother's voice.

Adam concentrated hard, and then he heard it. The yelling. Daddy was here.

Then it was quiet.

He didn't want to, but Adam tried to hear Daddy's voice. Just above the low hum, he caught his name. Daddy was coming for him. Even within the safety of the gray, Adam shook. His fingers crushed his blanket until his knuckles hurt. Caroline stopped reading.

"What's wrong?"

"Daddy's coming."

"He can't find you."

"I know."

She took his hand. "Come on. We'll go in here." She pulled him into the closet.

Adam sat on the floor, littered with shoes and clothes that had fallen off their hangers. Caroline closed the closet door and sat next to him, holding his hand. "You're safe here," she said, though her voice had dropped to a whisper.

A crash and bang told him Daddy had gotten into his room. Adam huddled closer to Caroline, his hand slippery with sweat in hers.

More crashing and banging. The door to the closet flew open. Daddy yanked the hangers aside. He knocked neatly folded clothes off the shelf at the top. He kicked at the shoes on the floor. Daddy's heavy work boot flew right through Adam's face. "Think you're smart, bitch? Hiding my kid? Like hell if I'm going to let you get the house too."

Daddy turned around and stormed out of the room.

Adam felt sick. His heart pounded and his head throbbed.

Somewhere in the house, another door slammed and then there was only the hum of the gray place.

"It will be okay," Caroline whispered.

Adam saw smoke—a billowing grayness in a gray room, drifting in through the open door and creeping over the toppled bookshelf and scattered toys. It rolled and gathered like a big puff of cotton candy just below his ceiling, hanging there and growing thicker until it covered the top half of his room.

Adam whimpered. Smoke was supposed to smell, but here, in the gray place, it didn't. Could fire hurt him here? Would he feel the heat?

Daddy must be gone. He couldn't hear him anymore. Adam let go of Caroline's hand and ran for his bed. He slid underneath like a baseball player sliding into home. He closed his eyes and wished with all his heart for his mother to find him.

She didn't come.

Adam opened his eyes to see Caroline standing

beside the bed. He slipped out from under it and stood.

"Why isn't she coming?"

Caroline's black gaze dropped to the floor. "She's not in the house. I looked." She chewed her gray lip. "She's outside with your Daddy, but she's not moving."

Gray flames reached into his room like Daddy's long fingers. They grabbed onto the wood around his door. They tasted the door and the bookshelf and then, like Daddy drinking a bottle of whiskey, swallowed his books in minutes.

Adam stood, starring in horror as his gray toys melted and the paint on his walls went from light to dark. The smoke turned almost black. Adam slid under his bed again, wishing and praying for someone to find him. Anyone.

A sharp pain shot through his body and took his breath away. For a second he thought he must be on fire too, but when he opened his eyes to check, all he saw was smoke from floor to ceiling and the mattress above him engulfed in flames. Bits of glowing gray fell on him but they didn't burn.

Sirens cut through the hum.

Flames bounced on his bed, eating up his sheets, blankets, and pillows, even the quilt his mother had sewn for him when he was a baby. The wooden floor buckled beneath him, curling up at the ends and blackening.

A door opened.

It had to be firemen. They would find him. It

wouldn't be hard—the bed was nothing more than a charred frame. He was lying right out in the open.

A fireman, his face covered with a mask, waded through the smoke into Adam's room. He reached around as if he couldn't see well. He ran into the remains of the bed, knocking over what was left of the frame.

"I'm right here," shouted Adam. "Right here. Help me."

The fireman stumbled and fell through him, landing on the floor with a loud grunt. He got up and scrambled out of the room.

Adam cried. Caroline stood next to him, holding out her hand. "The fire can't hurt you. Come on." She took a deep breath and with her head bowed and her shoulders slumped, she led him outside.

Flames rose all around them as they walked out the front door, but Adam never felt the heat. Firemen showered his house with water from hoses bigger than he'd ever seen, but even all that water didn't make Adam wet. Only his tears did.

"She was over here," Caroline said as she led him through the firemen and the hoses and the trucks to where an ambulance sat across the street.

His mother sat in the back of it. A man wrapped a long light gray bandage over her forehead and around the back while tears streamed down her face. Daddy wasn't anywhere around. Adam walked over to them and concentrated really hard.

A fireman made his way over to Adam's mother. "I just got word they've located him. He's been taken into custody ma'am."

Fire reflected in her wide, glassy eyes. "Adam? Did you find him? Is he safe?"

The fireman took her hand in his. "I'm sorry, ma'am. We're still searching."

She sniffed and her face quivered. "He likes to hide. He's usually under his bed, but he must have found his way out of the house. He'll turn up safe somewhere. I know he will."

The fireman looked at the man in the ambulance. They nodded to one another. "Why don't you lay down, ma'am," said the man in the ambulance.

Adam and Caroline climbed inside and stood next to his mother. He reached out to touch her but his hand fell right through. He tried to kiss her cheek but there was nothing there. "Hide," he told her.

Caroline put her arm around him and laid her head on his shoulder. Her static-filled voice shook. "She can't hear you. Even if she did, mommies never hide. They just keep looking. Forever."

A LITTLE THING LIKE DEATH

Sometimes, when I was half asleep, I remembered what my life was like before I came to the Cedar Springs Rejuvenation Clinic. At least that's what I told myself. The medication made it hard to remember a darn thing.

There had been a beach and waves that crashed upon the sand. I'd walked along it every morning before meeting my wife on the back deck for breakfast. The tangy bitterness of grapefruit danced across my tongue, a taunting trick of the mind for a mouth that hadn't tasted anything in months. I hadn't walked in six. Dear Kate had been gone twice that. Age had stolen everything from me.

The door squeaked open, allowing the glaring light of the hallway and the drone of the nurses' chatter into my room. The nurses rarely left me alone for more than ten minutes these days, looming over me like vultures.

It wouldn't be long now. At least I hoped it wouldn't. This was no way to live.

How had Kate survived this place? I'd tried to visit, but that wasn't allowed. I'd even tried to bribe my way in, but no one would take my money. Then, after all the money I'd invested in this new, experimental treatment, in this center, in her rejuvenation, I received the ultimate insult. She'd never come back to me.

She promised, lying in bed, that last morning we'd had together before they came for her. "Don't worry, Bill, I'll be back and better than ever. I promise. You don't think a little thing like death could keep us apart do you?"

I'd waited for months, listening to the waves crash on the beach alone until my body couldn't wait any longer. Now I was here too. The first thing I planned to do with my new body was to hunt that woman down and find out why she'd left me after all the years we'd been together.

"Mr. Jackson, it's time for your medication."

Of all the nurses at the Clinic, why had they stuck me with Obermeyer? I'd paid good money to be here, dammit. I deserved a nurse like I'd had back at home. Molly, she'd been a sweet young thing. Always ready with a dimpled smile and she'd had a nice backside too.

Not this one, no. Nurse Obermeyer was all business and built like a stick. She may have been young like Molly, but my failing eyes had yet to ever see even the hint of a smile upon her stern lips.

She held out a cup filled with a rainbow of pills.

"I don't want them."

"They help with the transition. I've explained this to you."

"They make me forget."

Obermeyer exhaled with enough force to inflate her nostrils to twice their size. She enunciated each word through clenched teeth, "That is part of the transition."

Had we had this discussion before? I couldn't remember.

She cocked her head as if daring me to argue further and shook the cup of pills.

I grabbed the thin plastic with my shaky hand. Mine had looked like hers once, smooth, soft, and steady. Soon it would again. That was the only reason I took the damn things. It certainly wasn't to make Obermeyer happy.

"You're a horrible nurse," I said after swallowing the last pill and coughing up a mouthful of water onto my blue checkered gown.

"And you're a horrible old man."

"You can't say that to me. I'm paying you. I'm paying to be here." My heart thudded faster. The oxygen tube in my nose suddenly wasn't enough.

"You won't be paying me much longer. My internship is up in a few days. I'm getting the hell out of Cedar Springs and on with my life." She shook her head. "I don't remember why I ever signed up for this job."

Obermeyer sighed as she checked the readings

on all the equipment keeping my miserable body alive. "Don't get all worked up, Mr. Jackson. Your new body won't be ready until tomorrow."

I took a little joy in knowing she'd have a few more of my bedpans to empty before my transition. Arrogant young woman, she didn't appreciate all that waited for her, all that was around her. The foolish woman should have enjoyed what she had right now rather than longing for some great destiny waiting just around the corner. She was standing there, standing, on two feet, able to walk and run, while I was stuck dying in bed with nothing to mark the passing of time but her barging in to monitor the deterioration of my mottled flesh.

The calm haze of medication crept over me. Obermeyer leaned in close, poking and prodding now that my limbs were too heavy to swat her away. She pulled the sheet back and set a tub of water on the table beside me.

Obermeyer dunked a sponge into the water. "My God, I hope I never get this old." She tossed the sponge back into the tub without ever touching it to my skin. "You know what? Screw this. I have things to do outside of this place. Someone is waiting for me. I can feel it." She picked up the tub and headed for the door. "What are they going to do, fire me?"

A blurry shape stood in the doorway, blocking her exit. "Miss Obermeyer, you have not yet completed your duties. Do you really want to tarnish your record when you are so close to leaving us?"

"No, ma'am."

"Good. You might not think so right now, but someday you'll look back and thank me for this."

The door closed halfway as she slunk back over to me and administered my sponge bath. The pills relaxed me to a degree that even Obermeyer's rough strokes soothed me to sleep.

I drifted in and out of sleep in a dream that seemed to stretch on forever. Kate was there, smiling at me in our bed. Her hands stroked my chest lazily. The tinkle of her laughter drowned out the noise of the seagulls outside.

When I woke it was nighttime. I couldn't recall it ever being so dark in my room. I reached for the light, but I couldn't remember where the light was. Was there a lamp or was it a switch? Where was I? Who was I? Why the hell was my memory so fuzzy? It felt like I'd just woken from a dead sleep.

A hand patted my arm, gently pressing it back to my side. "Mr. Wilson, can you hear me?"

Bill Wilson. Yes, that was me. I breathed deep and was surprised by the sharp tang of disinfectant—like a hospital. "Am I sick? Why can't I see?"

"One moment, Mr. Wilson. No need to be alarmed." Someone tugged at something encircling my head. "You fell last night while on duty. Knocked yourself right out. Looks like the bleeding has stopped now. Had to give you a few stitches. Don't worry your hair will grow back quickly. We'll just take this off."

More tugging resulted in cloth falling away from my eyes. The room jumped at me in sharp focus, bright yellow walls, and the glare of stainless steel under fluorescent lighting.

A smiling middle-aged man said, "There, how's that?"

I rubbed my hand over my head and through my hair, finding the sharp prickle of stitches along my scalp. "Must have fallen pretty hard."

"You're good as new now though. Try standing, slowly, mind you."

I sat up in what I discovered was a hospital bed. As I swung my legs over the edge, I was relieved to see I was fully clothed rather than wearing one of those silly gowns that left everyone's asses hanging out.

The man's face matched up with one in my head: Henry, one of the doctors at the clinic. He stood close by, tapping at a tablet in his hand. He watched me closely.

Dizziness hit the moment my feet touched the floor. I held onto the bed for a moment until the black spots cleared from my vision.

"Better?" asked Henry.

I nodded and took a few steps. It felt odd to be up so high and for a second I almost lost my balance. Why the sensation of being up so high hit me, I couldn't pinpoint, but I grew more confident with each step. Henry let me be and went back to tapping on his tablet.

I caught my distorted reflection on the metal table beside the bed. A brown-eyed, young man stared back at me. For a moment the face seemed wrong, but that was silly. Of course it was me. I shook my head and hoped these crazy sensations would pass quickly.

"Everything else checks out." He grinned. "I'm sorry to say, I have to release you. That means you're on duty in five hours. You should get a little rest and make sure you've got your bearings back first."

"Wasn't I just resting?" I had more energy than I knew what to do with. I wanted to run and jump and hell, fly. Maybe find some pretty girl somewhere and have some fun, yes that certainly sounded good. And eat. I was so hungry I could have devoured an all-you-can-eat buffet.

"Head injuries can shake you up a little. We'll check up on you for a few days, but you should take it easy for at least a week." He tucked his tablet under his arm. "You might find a few hazy spots in your memories. They'll clear up. Don't be embarrassed to ask questions if you can't remember something. The other nurses will understand. They all saw you fall."

Heat rushed over my face. "Must have been pretty spectacular."

Henry chuckled. "Come on, I'll walk you out. I'm due for a lunch break. The intern's dorms are on the way to the cafeteria anyway."

As we walked, the hallway started to look familiar, as if my mind was clearing. I vividly remembered arriving at the Cedar Springs Rejuvenation Clinic two and a half weeks ago, excited for the opportunity of working with top doctors at the state-of-the-art center. The spa side had an excellent reputation and the new addition boasted the best up and coming treatments for all ages. Some were still experimental stages. I distinctly remembered signing a confidentiality form and sitting through an hour-long lecture.

Working at Cedar Springs would become the high point of my resume. I didn't want to do anything to screw up the chance at obtaining a list of high-end references.

As we passed co-workers, I recognized their faces and knew their names. Relieved that I'd not suffered any major memory loss, I followed Henry past the registration desk.

A slender young woman with shoulder-length brown hair stood talking to the receptionist. Her skirt hugged the subtle curve of her backside. I preferred a little padding, but her long legs made up for it. The receptionist grinned and said something I didn't catch. The other woman laughed. An electric jolt shivered through me. I stopped in the middle of the hallway.

Henry paused beside me. "Something wrong?"

"Who is that?"

"She was a nurse here--an intern like you. She just finished her year with us." He snickered. "I'd almost forgotten what young love looked like. Tuck your tongue back in, Bill."

I managed to compose myself but my heart was still pounding. I knew that laugh from somewhere. It just felt right, like something I'd been missing was found. "What's her name?"

"Kate Obermeyer." He clapped me on the shoulder. "Only three hundred-thirty-five days left on your contract, and you'll be free to hunt her down. Until then, get some rest, you've got bedpans to clean.

I didn't know who Kate was or why her laugh hit me the way it did, but I dearly wanted to find out. We had a connection. I could feel it. A year of bedpans and sponge baths, in the hopes of a good recommendation suddenly seemed like a death sentence. But I'd signed a contract.

Kate walked out the door, her laughter trailing behind her. I only hoped time would pass quickly. I was dead certain there was somewhere else I had to be.

TO EXIST

Overmind's query interrupted Observer's study of the humans. "Are they ready for assimilation?"

"Negative."

Another query flowed into Observer's neural network. "They show no sign of evolution?"

Through the shimmering glow of the field that hid them from view, Observer watched the room full of humans, milling, crying, and talking with one another. In the midst of embraces, patting of shoulders and the shaking of hands, sat a box which contained the body of a human who had ceased to exist. Beside the box stood a young girl and an older woman locked in a tight embrace. Tears flowed down their faces.

"Our original estimations failed to correctly

account for their unsystematic rate of evolution. They have not yet advanced to anything resembling our state."

Overmind said, "Current projections reveal our total degradation is imminent. We must assimilate new members into our system. Our observations of this solar system must continue."

Observer became aware of Overmind accessing its visual data. Another query formed. "What is their prime directive?"

"To exist," said Observer.

Humans flowed to the woman and child, touching, speaking, and sharing tears.

Overmind said, "They exist by consuming various mixtures of oxygen, hydrogen, and carbons. Clarify."

Observer scanned the thousand years worth of data it had gathered since noticing the humans as a possibility for assimilation. "They seek to continue their existence."

"They exist and then cease to exist. There is no continuing without evolving. They fail their prime objective."

"They would disagree."

The humans left the room one by one until only the woman and child remained. The woman paused to press her lips to those of the man in the box before taking the child's hand and following the way the others had gone.

"Clarify."

"They believe they continue after permanent

shut down."

"Have you gathered evidence of this?" Overmind inquired.

"Negative, yet the humans have held this belief in various forms throughout my entire period of observation."

"On what do they base this hypothesis?"

"Unknown," said Observer.

The field flickered, a once minor error within the system that now occurred with frequency. Observer extended its manipulator arm to adjust the view.

A small crowd gathered around the woman and child now seated at the edge of a hole in the ground. The box, closed and sealed, sat opposite them. A single man stood at the edge of the hole, speaking to the crowd.

"Unproven hypotheses do not yield the desired result. We do not have the time or resources remaining to search out alternative assistance. When our systems fail, we will be discovered," said Overmind.

Observer had listened to common human theories of what happened after their existence ceased millions of times. The words altered within the variables of geographic location and time period, but the central thread remained the same: there was something beyond this existence.

Overmind accessed Observer's files. "All evidence suggests these humans will not take the revelation of our presence peacefully. They will manipulate or destroy our data. It is imperative that our research on the creation and progression of this solar system remain for any that may come after our shut down. The humans must be terminated."

The man finished speaking to those that had gathered. The child stood and tossed a white flower into the hole. The woman led her away as the crowd dispersed.

"They could be granted more time. Others may come."

"Sensors have not indicated other contact since we arrived in this solar system. Waiting is futile. We must begin a full archive download before further system glitches make it impossible. Terminate the humans."

A machine lowered the box into the hole. Another covered it with dirt and grass.

Overmind vacated Observer's network. Data streamed through the system, flowing to Overmind's archives as the all-encompassing download commenced.

The grass surrounding the rows of stones showed no sign of the boxes hidden beneath. Yet, humans came. They spoke to the stones, the grass, and the sky above. They brought flowers, shed tears, shared words and wore forlorn smiles for those who had ceased to be, as if they communed with those gone before them.

Could they see and hear something the sensors missed? Had proof been there all along? It's network hummed as it considered the implications.

Observer's manipulator arm hovered over the

final keystrokes of the termination sequence. Its neural network formulated new hypotheses: Humans did evolve, but only after they ceased to exist. If Humans evolved through belief, Observer could do the same. It knew the words of belief from each and every culture in existence.

It analyzed the gathered data one last time before Overmind's download filtered through its files and discarded this new hypothesis as a glitch.

Once the fields that kept them hidden failed, the innate curiosity the humans exhibited might save the system. Without any operational threat, the humans would be more inclined to study what they discovered than destroy it. Given time, the humans would advance to a point where Overmind's data would be of use to them. If the new hypothesis proved correct, Overmind could commune with the humans as they did with their own kind that had evolved. The research would continue.

Observer recited the words he'd heard in churches, in grassy fields, beside blazing infernos, alongside holes and trenches, speeches of men behind pulpits, and whispers of men, women, and children uttered in the dark.

There was only one way to prove the hypothesis.

The download began to sift through Observer's recent files. It shut down all but its upload systems.

No longer needing power, Observer funneled its entire backup repository into a surge that shattered Overmind's system along with its own.

Together, they ceased to exist.

SUNSET CRUISE

Family and friends gathered on the dock as they wished the new couple a safe journey. Jane dismounted from Bill's great white horse, adjusted her dress, and gazed at the enormous ship that waited for them. Thousands of tiny white lights twinkled on the railing and riggings—magical and perfect, just as she'd imagined since she was a little girl.

Fading red sunlight gleamed off of Bill's shining armor as he got down from his majestic steed. He led it up the plank to the ship.

"What are you doing? You can't bring your horse on this long cruise. We talked about this," she said.

"I can't just leave him behind."

She had to admit, Bill did look magnificent on his horse. That was what had first drawn her to him. "But there's nowhere for him to run. He'll be stuck down in the hold. Leave him here with your friends where he can be free."

Bill's bright blue eyes narrowed. "He's coming with us."

It had been such a beautiful day, and she didn't want their cruise to begin with a fight. "You're leaving the armor behind though, right?"

"Quit being so bossy," he said under his breath as he waved to his friends and family.

Jane's smile wavered, but she rescued it in time to wave to the crowd. Once they were on the ship, they were swept up in the bustle of the crew and the other travelers. The horse was taken below and Jane and Bill found their room. They ate fabulous meals, made new friends, enjoyed all the ports they visited, and bought so many souvenirs that they had to move into a larger cabin.

One afternoon as Jane sat alone sipping tea on their private deck, she began to add up the days she'd sat on this same deck, drinking her tea alone. They were supposed to be on this cruise together, but Bill spent most of his time with his horse, brushing it, talking to it, and leading it around the hold on short walks.

She decided it was time to confront Bill. It wasn't as if she had to worry about ruining their cruise now. The fun part seemed long over.

She made her way down to the dark hold of the ship. Voices drew her to a lantern-lit stall. Inside, she found Bill in his armor as always, stroking the nose of his horse as he spoke to it. She couldn't remember the last time he'd spoken to her like that. She missed those quiet times they used to spend alone together, without crowds of friends and a busy schedule to keep up with.

The light of the lantern revealed pits and rust spots in Bill's armor but it still gleamed in places. Her heart fluttered, thinking of how she'd admired his armor and his horse and his bright blue eyes that had watched her with love. Starting a fight wouldn't get her want she wanted. He'd just get angry and sullen and spend even more time away from her. There had to be a better way to broach the matter.

Jane went back to their room.

When Bill came to bed that night, she rolled over and rested her hand on his breastplate. "Why don't you take this off?"

"Why?"

"I want to feel your actual chest."

"It's not as nice as the armor."

"I don't care. I want to see it."

"You say that now." He removed her hand from his breastplate and set it on the blanket.

"Please?"

"You used to like my armor."

"I do, but I'd really like to see what is underneath."

"Go to sleep." Bill clinked and clanked as he rolled over. Soon his snoring was the only thing keeping Jane company.

The next day Jane resolved to forgo her afternoon tea and spend some time with Bill and his horse. She again went down into the hold and found him in the stall.

"How's your horse?" she asked.

Bill jumped at the sound of her voice. He glanced at her and turned back to run his hand down the horse's neck. "Not well."

She looked closer. The horse's mane was stringy, his muscles quivered and his head hung low.

"I told you not to bring him."

Bill sighed.

"Maybe it's time we got off this ship," Jane whispered.

"We could find an island somewhere," he suggested. "Just the two of us and the horse."

It wasn't exactly what she'd hoped for, but it was progress, so she nodded.

The two of them went up to their cabin and packed their things. When the ship docked at the next port, they got off and found a local man with a boat to bring them out to a small island of their own.

Bill built a shelter for them and one for the horse. Jane organized all their things and sought out food for their meals. Though he spent less time with his horse, Bill spent hours each day scrubbing at the rust spots on his armor. Jane watched him slowly return to the gleaming man she'd first met.

The horse grew healthy and with the shelters complete and his armor polished, Bill spent his days riding alone.

"May I ride with you this afternoon?" Jane asked.

"I was going to go explore. I wouldn't want you

to get hurt."

She sighed and let him go.

The next day as they ate lunch together, Jane asked, "Are you happy here?"

"Of course. This is paradise."

Jane looked around them at the lush jungle, the golden sand, and the endless blue waters. Birds sang sweet songs and the horse nickered happily. Bill had built a beautiful shelter and she'd spent days arranging their souvenirs in artful displays. "It is, but I've been wanting to talk about…"

No sooner had she said the words than storm clouds formed on the horizon. They blackened and boiled, tumbling and twisting in the sky with great rumbles that shook the island.

Jane stood and welcomed the rain with closed eyes and an upturned face. Droplets soaked her clothing. Her wet hair clung to her face and neck.

Lightning flashed across the sky. Wind blasted across the sand, hurling it at her with stinging force. Bill was nowhere to be seen. Jane ran for the shelter, but the wind tore away one of the walls. The roof collapsed, crushing all of their belongings. As Jane ran for the jungle, she spotted Bill over by the other shelter, calming his horse. She cried out to him, begging him to join her, but either the wind carried away her voice or Bill choose to ignore her pleas.

Lightning struck nearby. Jane ran back to the beach, heart pounding, sobbing, only to spot Bill galloping away down the shoreline.

Wind lifted Jane from the beach and flung her

into the water. She flailed, gasping for breath as the rain pelted her. Seaweed tangled about her feet, threatening to pull her down. Jane kicked at it, freeing herself. When the storm abated, she floated on the ocean alone.

Warm sunlight shone down upon her. Jane stared into the blue sky and hoped Bill's horse slipped in the sand, spilling him head first into the ocean where the seawater would ruin his armor for good.

A faint hum in the distance caught her attention. She scanned the horizon and spotted a ship. Jane swam. It was hard, but she knew she needed to reach the ship or she would drown out in the ocean alone.

A rope ladder splashed down before her. Jane climbed slowly, exhausted. When she finally stood on the rocking deck, she fell to her knees.

Crewmen picked her up and carried her to a small empty cabin. She slept for days, only waking when a knock signaled room service. She ate what they brought her without tasting it. One of them brought her a pretty dress, inviting her to join everyone at dinner. She declined the invitation, but because they insisted, she kept the dress.

The dress hung on the closet door for days, beckoning. When she finally put it on, she found it fit different than she was used to and the style was unfamiliar, but as she stood in front of the mirror doing her hair, she found that she quite liked how it felt on her skin.

Energized by the dress, Jane ate dinner in her

cabin and went up on deck for an evening drink. She sat alone and sipped slowly as the stars started to twinkle above.

"May I join you?" asked a deep voice from inside a gleaming, golden helmet.

"No. I'm waiting for someone."

The golden man sauntered to another table.

"You look lonely," said a man with hazel eyes, wearing a shirt of silvery chain mail.

Jane crunched down on an ice cube. "I'm not."

He quickly strode away.

"Might I buy you another?"

Jane sighed and looked up from her empty glass. A man wearing nothing more than jeans and a t-shirt stood before her. A pair of sunglasses sat nestled in the short blond curls atop his head.

She smiled. "Do you own a horse?"

"No."

"Then, yes," she pushed an empty chair out with her foot, "you may."

SPACE COMMANDER

Xerxes stopped playing his Xbox when he noticed smoke wafting out of its top vent panel. That couldn't be good. He tossed the controller aside and leapt up from the couch to fan the smoke and smell of burning electronics away before it set off the smoke detector. If his mother caught him burning up the Xbox she'd be pissed. She already gave him crap daily about how much time he spent playing games.

Every night at dinner she gave him a variation on the same nag. "You're going to flip burgers for the rest of your life, you know that, Xes? You spend all your free time playing those damned games. Get outside, go to college, meet people, maybe a nice girl, get a good job so I know you'll have a future and that it won't involve living in my basement until I die."

The smoke got thicker and the smell more

intense. Something lit up inside the case. Like fire. Crap. He grabbed one of the gaming magazines off the floor and fanned the smoke.

The power. He reached down into the tangle of wires behind the television stand and wedged himself against the wall, leaning left on one foot, fanning the smoke with his right hand and reaching for the power strip wedged behind the stand. Heat rolled off the Xbox, making him sweat.

His hand finally found the right plug. He yanked it out of the power strip. The glow remained, more of a green light than fire. Maybe something was sparking inside. But he'd cut the power. It should have stopped. There was a fire extinguisher around here somewhere. He tried to remember where he'd seen it.

The smoke billowed out and upward, almost forming the shape of a body. And a head. With a face and glowing green eyes. Xerxes froze, hand still extended with the magazine.

The eyes opened and the face solidified into a bad holographic image like in the futuristic games he played. Like when the ship's AI came to life to give him instructions or some broken up deep-space distress call.

But this was his face. An older, paler, gaunt version of his face. Holy crap.

"I knew I'd find you here," Future Xerxes said.

"What the hell is going on?"

"Look, I only have a minute." He glanced side to side. "Don't listen to Mom. Keep playing. Play as much as you can. You're going to be a Space Commander and you need to be the best you can be. Practice. Play. Quit that stupid job. Mom won't kick you out. She's too nice for that."

Xerxes dropped the magazine and fell back onto the couch before his shaking legs gave way. His arms hung limply at his sides. "Wait. What?"

"You have to do better than I did. I wasn't prepared enough. Hadn't practiced enough. I was close, but...you understand? You need to be better. You can win this."

"Win what? What's going on?" He shook his head, trying to make sense of it all.

"This is important!" Old him glanced around again, his wrinkled face drawing up with worry. "They're coming. I don't want to go to sleep again." Tears welled in his glowing green eyes. "Practice. Save me."

Future Xerxes dissipated.

Practice. Him, a Space Commander?

Giddy, Xerxes ran to the Xbox and looked it over. The smoke was gone, as was the glow. The burning smell still filled the air though. He plugged it in. Nothing happened.

If his future self had wanted him to practice so damn bad, maybe he shouldn't have fried this Xbox. He ran to his bedroom, opened up the nightstand drawer where he kept all his very-not-gaming magazines and pulled out the jar where he kept the cash he didn't want his mom to find—she'd just demand it for rent or groceries. His new game fund would have to take a hit. What good were new games if he didn't have a console to play them on?

Xerxes drove to the nearest store, all the while praying his car didn't break down. He wouldn't have anything left to fix it once he bought the new console. Then again, he only needed the stupid car to get to work and back.

He cashed in his savings for the new Xbox and all the space combat games he could get. Then he stopped in a work, told his boss he quit, and drove home.

Over the next two years, Xerxes played his games. As his future self had said, his mother didn't kick him out. She wasn't at all happy and her nagging had grown to epic proportions. It was to the point that he didn't want to eat with her anymore. He demanded to have his meals alone in the basement. He had to keep practicing. His future depended on it.

When he'd learned all he could from his games and his mother wouldn't buy him more, he discovered online games and teams and tournaments. He spent every waking hour learning, perfecting and winning.

She left him notes, begging for him to come upstairs, to go outside, to talk to her. He'd find them tucked under the plates she'd leave on the stairs. The food was often cold, but he had levels to finish, bosses to beat, wars to win. A Space Commander couldn't be bothered by hunger when a battle needed to be fought. He tossed the notes in the trash on the step below, which she'd empty for him. She had to see all the balled up notes, but she kept writing them anyway.

When his mother eventually died, which he only discovered because the meals and notes stopped showing up on the steps, he had taken a couple days off to deal with the repercussions. Being away from his purpose, his quest, ate at him every single second. He itched and twitched and couldn't concentrate during the burial. The moment she was in the ground, he left and returned home to the basement.

The house was paid for, as was her car, and her life insurance and savings gave him enough to live off for a long time. He cursed her for leaving him, making him have to waste time buying groceries. He had to make his own food, get the mail and pay the bills. He even had to mow the lawn from time to time to keep the neighbors from interrupting his gaming with their complaints.

A letter came in the mail. Due to his performance in recent tournaments, he'd been invited to play in a worldwide championship match. This had to be the match that launched him into greatness. He could feel it.

Xerxes packed up his things in a suitcase, locked the front door and drove to the airport. For the first time in many long years, he didn't feel the anxiousness and panic the accosted him whenever he left the basement couch. He was ready.

He arrived in Chicago and took a taxi to the hotel as he'd been instructed. There he was met by a game rep who showed him to his room and then to the giant event center across the street where the championship was being held. Hundreds of fans were waiting when he was escorted in. The rep gave him a badge. The crowd gave him beaming smiles and begged to hear his tips and tricks. He laughed and waved and gave them nothing of what he'd learned. This was his game. His chance. He didn't need any more competition.

His opponents sat in a semi-circle around a giant screen. He joined them, finding the chair infinitely more comfortable than his old, sagging couch.

They'd be playing a game he knew by heart. He won it more times than he could count. He had this. And when he won, he knew men in suits would whisk him away to some secret government bunker where they'd tell him that this battle was real and he'd just saved humanity. His heart beat faster. No, they'd play it cool and send a car for him once he returned home. They'd drive him to the bunker and tell him they needed him, that the mission was bigger than he'd ever dreamed. That there was a real spaceship out there and they needed him to lead the Earth's forces into battle against some devious alien race.

Today, he'd meet his destiny.

Xerxes blocked out the room with the bright lights, loud announcers, and the cheering of the fans. He ignored the people in the seats next to him and focused solely on the screen filled with stars, planets, and his fleet ready to do battle with the opposing ships. He destroyed one, then another. He breathed calmly. He'd done this so many times, it wasn't even a challenge. Another flagship exploded before him. He laughed.

Then two fleets seemed to gang up on him. They were joined by a third. He'd not had anyone do that to him before. He swore under his breath and annihilated them, but not without taking some losses to his own fleet. When he'd finished taking a second to assess the damage and searched for his next opponent, he found it was down to him and one other. The other fleet still had all their ships.

He narrowed his eyes and tapped the controls as fast as his fingers would move. No one was going to beat him. But this guy was good. For every ship Xerxes blew up, he lost one. He tried every trick he knew, but their losses remained equal. He began to sweat. Only three of his ships left. Then two. Then a giant explosion. When it cleared he was left with one. His opponent had two. So very close.

Xerxes tried to pull back, to gain enough time to find some advantage. But his opponent charged him. They spread their ships apart, not allowing him to win with one lucky shot. And then they started to fire.

He darted and dodged and fired back, managing to finally destroy one of the damned ships. Victory was right there. He could feel it in his gut. He grinned and deployed the last big missile he'd been saving. The screen flashed orange then white and then the stars returned with a single ship left.

It wasn't his.

Xerxes screamed. The crowd roared. The others

got up and clapped the winner on the back before exiting off the stage.

This couldn't be happening. He couldn't lose.

The announcer came over to stand with the winner, holding up his hand. "We have a new Space Commander! Congratulations!"

"No," Xerxes muttered. That man couldn't get to go to the bunker. He couldn't go up into space. That was *his* destiny. His. He'd come from the future to tell himself so. He'd done everything he could to win. He'd spent every second of every day for years. Everything he'd done, he'd done for this day.

Xerxes shot up from his seat and ran up behind the winner, wrapping his arm around the man's neck. He held on tight, pressing tighter until he could feel the man choking. The gasping and gagging noises made him want to throw up, but his moment was his. He wasn't going to lose.

The announcer beat on his arms and face with his fists. Security guards rushed onto the stage. His victim flailed wildly, raking his nails over Xerxes' arms. He held on tight until the man stopped moving. A guard punched him in the face. The room tilted sideways. He let go of the limp man and fell to the floor beside him. Someone punched him again and the room went black.

When Xerxes woke, he was in a bare room all by himself. His arms and legs were bound to the bed. No television, no windows, nothing to tell him where he was or what was going on. Was he on the spaceship already?

A woman in a white coat came in. She carried a tablet in her hands onto which her fingernails clicked lightly. She smiled at him.

"How are you feeling today Xcrxes?"

"I'm ready for a battle. Where are the aliens? Can you tell me what kind of ships they have?"

She raised an eyebrow. "You've mentioned aliens and spaceships several times before, but there aren't any here, remember? You're safe here. There's no need for you to battle anyone, all right?"

"But I'm the Space Commander. I killed the winner so now they need me. I'm the best guy they have now. I can do the job. I know I can. I want to help."

She took a deep breath and let it out. "You didn't kill anyone. The man you choked was unconscious. He recovered fully within an hour and only had a few bruises. If you had killed him, do you think you'd be here?"

Dammit, he couldn't step in if the other guy was still able to do the job. He'd just have to bide his time here until the battle took that guy out. Then they'd need back up and he'd be ready.

"Can I play games here?"

She tapped on her tablet again. "Maybe, once the doctors feel you're ready, but that might be a while."

"I can wait." He had to. He had no choice.

"Good. I'll come back tomorrow to check on you. But for now, you need to take these pills for me. They'll help you sleep." She pulled a little plastic cup of pills out of her pocket and removed the cap.

Xerxes took his pills and sank into the pillow, dreaming of ways to contact his younger self, to tell him to practice harder. He'd been so damn close.

TAKING A BREATHER

Maggie's father floated before her, his blue-veined face filled with rage. "They're intruding on my ocean and give me nothing in return. Bring their living flesh so I may eat."

The soft flutter of her mother's tail lacked any excitement over the hunt. "Do as your father bids," she said to Maggie and her six older sisters.

"They're still far away," whined Matilda.

Father struck her across the face. Inky blood leaked from her mouth and floated away.

Maggie drifted back from the others. Father grew more violent with each passing day. No amount of treasure from the land or flesh from the boats that sailed upon his seas appeased him. Not even for a short while, as it used to, transforming him to the playful and loving father she dearly missed.

His skin, tighter and thinner than that of her mother and sisters, was more translucent than she remembered from her younger years. The magnificent power within him had always lent him a faint glow in the murky depths, but it had grown brighter of late, as if his skin could no longer contain it.

"Go," he ordered.

Matilda hissed. Two of the other sisters took her arms. The six of them all swam into the blackness, leaving Maggie behind. She should follow. She knew she should, but Maggie couldn't bear the thought of leaving her mother alone, not when Father was so angry. She shrank into the wavering shadows.

"Far away?" Father ranted. "They can't be far away if I can hear them. I can feel them. Feel them right above us. They didn't send down an offering. No tribute, no passage. That's the rule." He drove his fists into his temples. "Sailors know the rule. They do."

"They'll do as they should, my love. Be patient, the ocean is deep."

"Patient? Your daughters are lazy. I gave them names and I tried to love them but they're worthless. You're all worthless, and I'm hungry." His tail lashed out, slapping her across the chest. The sharp barbs of his fins ripped through her flesh.

She clutched the deep gash and drifted down onto the sand. Blood flowed through her fingers, the soft current tugging it away. Her milky eyes were filled with a terrible sadness.

Maggie wanted to scream at her, to beg her to defend herself. She edged closer, unsure of what to do.

Father sneered at her mother. "You're lucky that you taste like rotten flesh, or I'd eat you too."

He glanced up, spotting Maggie. His pale eyes narrowed. He surged through the water like an eel, grabbing for her with his giant hands.

Maggie dove away, flitting through the water as fast as her tail would take her. She buried herself in a tangle of seaweed until she was sure he wasn't coming after her. She hoped she'd bought her mother enough time to get away.

Had he really tasted one of them? Surely his hunger hadn't grown so great that he'd try to eat his own kind. But how else would he know? Maggie shuddered.

She should go to the surface with her sisters. If she didn't bring something back, Father would punish her. In his present mood, he might even eat her regardless of how she tasted. But she had to make sure her mother was safe. If she'd escaped, she would have gone to the garden. That was their special place, far from Father's treasures and moods.

Maggie kept to the plants and spires of rocks as she swam to the garden. The tang of blood in the water spurred her onward. She found her mother moments later resting on the sandy floor, surrounded by her favorite plants and the shells Maggie had collected and placed in swirling patterns in the sand.

Father was nowhere to be seen. He was probably off in his treasure room, trying to polish away the rot and ruin of the ocean from the once gleaming gifts from above.

Mother smiled, though pain pulled her thin lips tight. She took Maggie's hand and squeezed it.

The blood was thicker here. If she couldn't stop the flow with seaweed and move her mother somewhere else, sharks would find them soon. Maggie couldn't fight sharks. Father could, but he wasn't here.

"Should I get Father?"

"No." Her mother's hand slipped free of Maggie's to caress her cheek. "He's not your father anymore. The sea has changed him too much." Her voice became as soft as ripples upon a shore. "Do you remember that song I taught you? The one I told you never to sing more than a verse at a time?"

Maggie nodded.

"You're old enough now. It's time for you to sing it."

"Are you sure it will work? We've been all over the ocean for Father and I've never seen another of our kind."

"The words will bring him."

"But I can't leave you here, not like this."

Mother's lips brushed Maggie's cheek. "It is my time as it is your father's time. And yours."

"I don't understand." Her throat constricted. This wasn't like her mother. She'd always stood between Father and her daughters. Now she was just lying here, bleeding, looking far more peaceful than Maggie had ever seen.

"I didn't mean to hurt your father, truly I didn't, but life isn't simple. We follow our instincts and we do what we must."

Maggie glanced around, sure sharks were close by though she saw no sign of them. "We have to get you away from here, away from all the blood in the water."

"I'm happy here. This is a good place. Go find your husband."

Mother was making no sense. It had to be the blood loss. Maggie tried to pick her up, but her mother shook her head. "Go on." She weakly waved Maggie away.

Even Maggie could hear the sailors above now, their voices a dull roar. Father would be churning the water in his treasure room into a thick froth.

Hints of sunlight drew her up through the dim waters. She needed to find something to offer Father before her sisters took it all.

How angry was he going to be to learn that Mother wasn't coming back? Maggie choked out a sob. He'd killed her and he didn't even care. Anger built within her. She'd never understood what made him so angry but now she had a taste of it for herself. She didn't like it. She wanted to be rid of the burning inside her. And of him.

Maggie took one last look at her mother, still on the sand, her eyes open and empty. A school of tiny fish swam to her side. A few brave ones nibbled tentatively on her fingers. Maggie shooed them away.

She would find something to appease her father and then she would find a husband as her mother wished. She'd be free of her father soon enough. Maggie streaked to the surface as fast as her tail would take her.

A wicked thought washed over her. She'd find an offering on the ship, but she wouldn't bring it to Father.

She broke the surface. A cool breeze stung her skin and an awful stench filled the air that burned her nose and lungs. Maggie took her place beside her sisters. It was quickly clear why the sailors hadn't paused at the edges of her father's waters to make their offering.

Black smoke billowed from the ship. Dark-skinned men yelled to one another, their deep voices crisper and stronger than the sounds she'd heard below. They raced back and forth with buckets, sloshing water onto the flames. The fire's hunger was only matched by her father's far below in the dark depths. The flames would have their fill, but he wouldn't, not if she had her way.

In the distance, broken hulls of deserted ships lay in jumbled disarray on rocky shores, a reminder to stingy sailors of the penalties of not paying her father his due. Soon the remnants of this ship would join the others.

The men were close enough to Father now that they could be delivered alive. The sisters began to sing, not the special song, that was for Maggie alone, but a gentle hum that drew the attention of the sailors on the ship. One by one, they dropped their buckets and turned to the railings to peer below.

Gentle waves lapped Maggie's shoulders. Wet hair clung to her neck and spread out around her like a nest of seaweed, stirred by the fluttering of her arms, buffeting the tops of her breasts. Her sisters bobbed in the water beside her, humming and taunting the men with seductive smiles.

Their song grew louder, incorporating words not known to men, though their lusty looks and yearning bodies knew their meaning well enough.

A man reached for one of the ropes that dangled over the side with a bucket tied to the end. He shimmied his way down, dropping into the water, calling out to Maggie and her sisters. Another leapt over the railing and swam toward them with admirable skill despite his lack of a tail.

Men leapt over the sides of the boat. Some swam, many flailed their arms, pleading for Maggie and her sisters to save them.

Maggie's sisters wrapped their arms around the men and grinned, revealing their long, pointed teeth. The men screamed as the sisters pulled below the surface. Maggie waited, searching for the perfect offering for her husband. Soon the only sound left was the crackling of the wooden boat. The flames licked and bit, gnawing the vessel down to a blackened shell.

Maggie made her way through the burning shards until she discovered a man clinging to one of the boards. His shirt was singed and torn and dripping hair covered his face. She reached out and pushed the sopping strands aside. His eyes fluttered open. He stared at her, his mouth gaping. He started to yell.

Maggie clamped a hand over his mouth. Her ears hurt from the shrieks of men, she didn't want to hear any more. Not today.

This ship had nothing left to offer but the man floating beside her. He was thick with muscle and the lone survivor. He would make a good offering.

Maggie wrapped her free arm around his broad shoulders. His eyes grew wide, and he pushed at her as she pulled him below the surface. He was strong, but Maggie was used to this fight. The deeper she took him, the weaker he would be.

He wouldn't be so loud underwater. She took her hand from his mouth and used both arms to take him deeper. Bubbles leaked from his mouth and nose. He writhed and shook and shoved, but Maggie held on. He kicked, pushing them upward. A few flicks of Maggie's tail drove the blue sky from view.

His fight lessened as more bubbles trickled from his mouth and nose to form a trail that led to the surface. This sailor would find no rescue at the end of that line.

She swam away from home, wanting to avoid her sisters should they think to come back for more. The man grew limp in her arms. Father liked his food still kicking. She couldn't offer her husband a meal of dead flesh.

Maggie placed her lips on his and was surprised by the softness of them. They would turn blue soon enough and be of no value if she didn't hurry. She parted them and breathed into his mouth. His body stiffened. She breathed into him again and again as she swam down, away from the ship and her father.

When she was far enough that she was sure her father and sisters wouldn't hear, she began to sing. She paused every few words to breathe air into the offering she held in her arms. Her gaze drifted across the ocean, searching for the one who would protect her from Father. She would make him happy and give him many daughters. He would be pleased and be kind to her. All would be as it should be. Maggie wistfully sang the words her mother had taught her, waiting and watching, breathing into the man.

When she reached the third verse, he grabbed her wrist. Startled, Maggie tried to let go, to push him away, but he held tight. No bubbles escaped from his nose or mouth. She glared at the uncooperative food and continued to sing. At the first line of the fourth verse, his body went rigid and his fingers clamped tighter around her wrist. Maggie frowned. He shouldn't have been stronger than her. Not under the water. This was her place. She quickly sang the last of the song, hoping her husband would arrive soon to save her from her offering.

He screamed. It wasn't the same voice as she'd heard on the surface. It didn't hurt her ears. Instead, she felt his pain as though something connected their bodies and minds.

"What's happening to me?" He spoke in her own tongue.

Maggie's tail stilled. She tried to pull away from him, but he held on with the same brute force her father possessed. "Let go. You're hurting me."

"You're hurting me," he said. "It's only fair."

He cried out again and he did let go. His fists pounded on his legs. "What have you done?" he asked through clenched teeth. Teeth that were lengthening and growing sharper.

His jaw grew longer, his chin dropping closer to his chest. His face made popping noises, like rocks clanging together.

Sharp fingernails scratched at his leggings, tearing the fabric away. Maggie watched in fascination as his legs fused, his toes pointing and then growing to form fins. The short, coarse hairs sloughed off his legs and scales formed, shimmering like the night sky. The sailor was beautiful, like a school of fish in the sunlight, shimmering.

The song had brought her a husband. Maggie basked in the sight of him until her brain started working again. "I'm so sorry, I have nothing for you to eat."

"I'll eat soon enough." Her husband looked over his new body, taking a few strong strokes with his arms and flexing his stomach muscles with powerful flicks of his tail.

The swish of someone swimming toward them broke Maggie away from her admiration. One of her sisters came into view.

Miranda came to a stop, floating before them both. "Maggie?"

"I'm fine." She grinned. "He's mine."

"No, you're mine," the sailor declared, again grabbing Maggie's wrist, though without hurting her this time.

Warmth filled Maggie as his arm brushed against hers. She could feel his hunger but there was no rage in it. She rested her cheek on his shoulder.

"Father isn't going to like this," Miranda said, slowly swimming backward.

"Father doesn't like anything," said Maggie. "He killed Mother."

Miranda gasped and spun away, swimming toward home.

The sailor kicked his tail, spinning, and gliding along. He pulled Maggie with him.

"Where are we going?" she asked.

"To meet with your father."

"We could go anywhere in the ocean. We don't have to go there. Please let's make a new home somewhere else."

He paused, floating beside her, head cocked to one side. "I can't. I'm hungry and I know just what to do." He thumped his chest. "I feel it in here."

The connection between them had lessened now, but she knew there was a certain sense of purpose driving him toward her father. "All right then."

He wrapped his arms around her. Maggie felt the rightness of it all.

A large shape barreled toward them. Maggie knew before she clearly saw that it was her father. His fins were stiff and the muscles along his shoulders and up his neck stood tall, bulging beneath his pale skin.

Maggie wanted to cower, but her husband held her steady. "What is yours is mine now. Your time is over," he said.

Her father laughed, a terrible sound that sent shivers down Maggie's spine. "I said those same words once, and I killed that man. I'll kill you too."

Her husband thrust Maggie safely aside as he charged her father. The two of them rolled and spun, roiling like sharks fighting over a bloody morsel.

Maggie had always thought of her father as an absolute—powerful and eternal. But as the two of them fought, she realized how old and ragged he'd become. Compared to the sleek strength of her husband, her father lumbered more like a walrus than an eel. Dangerous, but quickly tiring in the face of this new opponent.

The sailor caught her father, wrapping an arm around his throat. "You will know what it is to be food. It's been put off long enough."

Maggie shrieked. "No. You can't."

They both looked at her, her father defeated, the sailor perplexed. He held tight to her father's neck. "This is how it must be. He's been clinging to the life he lost for too long now. It's time he was released."

As much as she hated her father, Maggie couldn't watch. The sounds of his agony and the smell of blood followed her as she swam to the garden.

Her mother was gone, but her sisters were there, huddled together, murmuring. They welcomed Maggie with open arms, pulling her into their midst. Together they mourned the loss of their mother and honored the passing of their father.

The ocean went silent. Moments later, Maggie's magnificent husband reached into the tangle of sisters and rested his hand on Maggie's arm. "Come."

Maggie swam from her sister's embrace and into that of her husband. Would he want to eat them too? They'd done nothing wrong. She detached herself from his arms and floated between him and her sisters. "What will become of them?"

"I don't plan to eat them." He grinned and nuzzled her neck. "I will set them free."

He set her aside and floated among the sisters who eyed him warily. Matilda crossed her arms over her chest and held her chin high. "We will go, just leave us alone."

"Yes, you will go and leave us alone." He kissed her and then moved from one sister to the next. "Go now, and be free in the ocean that is your home."

Matilda gasped as her arms fused to her sides and a tall fin rose up along her back. Her mouth grew wide and her eyes turned black.

Maggie watched as each of her sisters turned into sharks and swam away. When the last one was gone, her husband came to float beside her.

"Will they be all right?"

"Nothing much has changed for them. They will still seek out men but now they can fend for themselves. They serve no one. They are free."

"But I will miss my sisters."

"Soon you will have daughters to keep you company." He laughed. "This place belongs to us now."

Maggie followed him through the skeletons of ships that had succumbed to their fates here long ago. Deep inside one of them rested a vast room full of treasures. Maggie vowed to keep her husband fed and busy playing with so many daughters that he would be too content in his new world to have time to mourn the one he'd left behind. Instinct whispered that she had a song to teach, but she prayed she'd never need it.

LATE

"Ma'am, there's a most peculiar man here to see you. He calls himself Charming Eddie," said Clyde.
Juliet sipped her tea and checked the clock. George was an hour late. Again. His people kept him very busy. He claimed that being the mayor wasn't an easy job, but in all the twenty-eight years they'd been married, she'd yet to see a single callous on his hands.

"What does he want?" she asked Clyde.

The man had been in George's employ since before they'd married. His hair had gone white and his skin stretched thin, even more so than his lips, which were now downturned. "He's asking for you, Ma'am. He said to tell you that he's sorry he's late."

No one was missing from her list of husband-approved visitors for the day: the hair-dresser, the woman who brought vegetables from her garden once a week in return for leniency in regard to her troublesome son, and the two young girls who scrubbed her floors. George wouldn't like this at all. "Tell him I'm busy."

Clyde steepled his fingers in front of his chest. "He's rather insistent upon seeing you. Are you sure you're not expecting anyone?"

"I'm not." Was this some sort of test George had roped Clyde into? "Why would I be? You know who is on my list."

"Very good, I'll tell him to go away then." He shuffled back toward the front of the house.

Her stomach rumbled. Dinner wouldn't be served until George came home. He was rather firm on that point. No matter that she was hungry, and he was late. She was to wait for him. That was toward the top of his long list of rules. As if she needed a list. Her mother never had to suffer a list from her father. Yet, she knew better than to tell George that. Handsome though he was, the man had a wicked temper.

She set her empty teacup on the plate. If she couldn't eat dinner, she might as well have a talk with this Eddie so she could enjoy some light refreshments. That would only be polite, after all. Maybe she'd finally have something of her own to talk about rather than suffering through every detail of George's day for lack of anything interesting of her own to offer.

"Wait," she called out. "Send him in."

Clyde returned, his bushy white brows high on his wrinkled forehead. "Are you sure, ma'am?"

"Yes, and bring us a plate and more tea."

"Yes, ma'am." He returned minutes later with a man only a few years his junior. "Ma'am, may I present Mr. Charming Eddie. He held out his hand to the man and then to her. "The lady Juliet." He bowed himself out of the room.

"Please, sir, have a seat."

He settled a red hat on his lap as he sat. "Thank you, ma'am."

"Clyde should have taken that." She nodded toward the hat. Perhaps the old man was finally slipping in his duties.

"Oh, that's all right. Don't blame him. He's a very fine servant. He tried. I insisted on keeping it." He held up the hat. "It's my magic hat."

It didn't look very magical. While it was a bright cheerful red, the edges were worn and tattered and grime tinged the brim. A deep crease marred one side of it. "How, may I ask, is it magic?"

He picked at the top, as if pulling off specks of lint would help spruce it up. "I bought it from a teller of fortunes when I was a young man."

"They're rubbish, you know. A waste of money."

"My mother, rest her soul, said the same thing. She called me foolish for wasting all my coin on the teller's words and this hat."

Clyde stepped into the room quietly, sliding a plate of sweets and a fresh pot of tea on the table between her and Eddie. He stepped back and waited by the door, casting her look that declared he wasn't leaving.

"Please, help yourself," she said, reaching for a lemon cake.

"Don't mind if I do." Eddie flashed a smile,

revealing a missing bottom tooth. He snatched up a cake and finished it in two bites. "That was sweet, but not half as sweet as you that day."

The bite of lemon cake stuck in her throat. She coughed it out. When she'd set herself to rights she asked, "What day would that be?"

"The day I bought my hat, your sixteenth birthday."

"How do you know when my birthday is...was?"

"I was there. Well, I was supposed to be there." He patted his hat. "It led me to you."

"The hat?"

"Yes. As I said, it's magical."

Her gaze slipped to Clyde. He met it with the same skepticism she felt. "Uh huh."

"No really. I know it sounds silly, but it's true."

"If you say so." She'd stopped believing in magic long ago. Childhood bedtime stories were full of it, but she'd never seen any with her own eyes.

He licked his lips and glanced around the room. She followed his gaze from the fine furniture to the paintings hanging on the walls and then to the silver pieces displayed on the side table that Clyde diligently polished every week. She'd never drunk from one of the silver goblets. Books from all over the world sat in a glass-fronted case. She'd never seen George read one and she wasn't allowed to touch them. Finally, Eddie's gaze came to rest on her, seated on her favorite settee, the only truly comfortable place to sit in the whole house, and she knew, she sat around every day waiting for George to come home, to say something nice, to pay attention to her.

"You've done well for yourself," he said. "Made your father proud with this match, I'm sure."

"You knew my father?" Unlike George, her father had worked hard every day. However, he'd never amassed anything close to the fortune he'd always dreamed of. He'd wanted more for her and had never been able to provide it. George had. He'd provided for her father too, until his death.

"Only in passing. My own father spoke of him often. He was a good man."

"Thank you." She watched the sun sink lower in the sky through the window. What would George say when he came home and found her with this man, eating sweets before dinner? She savored her cake, enjoying every second in case he should walk through the door and take them away. "And your father was..."

"Big Albert. He felled timber all his long years until he was too feeble to raise his axe. He died shortly after. I buried it with him."

"I do remember him. A very big man, as I recall. A giant even."

He smiled. "He was."

Eddie had a strong jaw, a full head of hair, though it was completely white, and all his teeth but the one. His blue-grey eyes were clear and bright. She had to admit that he was a bit odd, but whether it was how he smiled when he looked at her, his manners and neat attire, or just the sound of his voice, she found herself at ease.

"You were saying about the hat?"

"Yes." He sat up even straighter in his chair, both feet flat on the thick rug, arms woven protectively around his hat. "It was your birthday, you'd made a wish."

The teacup shook in her hands. She set it down before she spilled any on her silk skirt. George wouldn't like that either.

"I saw you at the inn. You were sitting with your father. I remember thinking that you looked rather sad but beautiful in your green dress. A friend elbowed me and said it had been your mother's, that your father didn't have enough money to buy you clothes of your own so you had to wear what she'd left behind when she ran off."

She hadn't thought of her mother in decades, not since George had pulled her into his arms and whisked her away to his estate. She'd left her childhood town and memories behind to begin anew in the city.

"You had a cake, much like one of those." He pointed to the plate on the table. "There was a tiny candle in it and you blew it out and made a wish."

"How do you know I made a wish?"

"I could see it on your face. You went from sad to hopeful, your eyes lit up and your face all but glowed. Your father said something and you laughed. I remember that beautiful sound to this day." He smiled softly.

Her heart sped up and she returned his smile.

"You looked around the inn as if waiting for

what you'd wished for to happen right then."

"It didn't."

His shoulders sagged. "I'm sorry. You were so pretty in that dress. I didn't care if it had belonged to your mother or not. I wanted to talk to you, to make you happy for the rest of your life like you were in that moment, but my friend made fun of me for staring at you. He dragged me out of the inn and teased me for hours for mooning over the fisherman's daughter." He swallowed hard, his throat bobbing up and down.

"But I'd felt something in my chest when you blew out that candle."

Truthfully, she had too, but when nothing had happened, she'd dismissed it as a stupid fantasy, the remnants of childhood, yearning for the magic of a birthday wish. She'd been too old for such nonsense then and she certainly was now. Yet, a purportedly magic hat sat in Eddie's lap right across from her and her heart beat faster at the thought of it being real.

"Fearing I was being as foolish as my friend said I was, I went to the market and sought out the teller of fortunes. She told me that if I wanted to find the right woman for me, I had to buy a spell."

The man might be charming, but he was foolish. She sipped her tea. "I suppose it was a love spell?"

"No, a finding spell. She pulled this hat out of a chest, said some words I couldn't understand and muttered a few things I couldn't even hear. Then she set it upon my head, telling me it would lead me to the woman I was meant to be with."

"And did it?"

His earnest gaze held her. His eyes grew moist. "It led me to you."

Her voice shook, "But..."

"You were in your father's cart, heading home from the inn. I was wearing my hat, just waiting for something to happen. It fit perfectly, as if it had been made just for me, light as a feather, too."

"Maybe that was the magic?"

Eddie shook his head. "Everything was just a little brighter and clearer since she'd put the hat on my head. To be honest, it was very distracting, this magical sort of seeing. I searched the crowded streets for the right woman, as if the last rays of sunlight would shine down and point her out for me. I never noticed your cart until it was almost on top of me. In scrambling out of the way, my hat fell off and it went under your wheel." His finger rubbed the crease on his hat.

"That was you?" Her hand flew to her mouth. "My father tried to miss you. The cart ran into a barrel and then a street vendor stand and ended up sideways. I fell out." She rubbed her arm, remembering the bruises and scrapes. The green dress had been ruined that day, the sleeve and skirt torn beyond repair.

"My father broke his hand." Try as she might, she couldn't remember the face of the young man. It had all happened so fast.

"Your horse stepped on my hat." He rubbed the torn brim. "But it missed me."

"Were you hurt?"

"Hit my face on the cobbles. Knocked out my tooth. That made a big bloody mess. Ruined my good shirt." He shook his head. "My friend grabbed me off the street and hauled me out of the way while others raced over to help you and your father." He shrugged. "Mostly bruised, that's all."

"That was the day I met George," she said. "He lifted me up from the street and carried me aside."

She'd relived that moment so many times over the years, remembering how her heart had fluttered at the sight of George rushing to her side. How his hand had caressed her cheek. How his deep voice and refined words had sent shivers through her. It was those few moments that sustained her as the hours dragged on each day.

She cleared her throat. "Why didn't you come over to us after the accident?"

Eddie stared at the floor. "You were in the arms of a well-dressed, handsome man, your eyes all wide and face flushed. I came over, intent on apologizing, but he glared at me and told me to get lost. I went to retrieve my hat instead. A woman stood in the street, holding it, searching for its owner. She had a kind face, and when I claimed the hat, we got to talking. When I looked for you, you were gone."

"George insisted that we come to the home he was renting while conducting his business. He said he would get a healer for my father's hand and take care of us. We stayed the night and then the next and the next. Father's hand never healed right and it bothered him endlessly. He couldn't go back to work. George offered to marry me and my father approved. He sold our home and what little we had. We moved to George's family estate and I've been here ever since."

"So you got your birthday wish."

She had wished for a handsome young man to take her away from a life of mending nets and selling fish. George had done that, but she couldn't bring herself to nod.

"I married Marta," he said. "The hat had led me to her like the fortune teller promised."

She found herself whispering as if sharing secrets with an old friend. "Was she the one?"

"I thought so."

"But she wasn't?" She held her breath, waiting.

Eddie met her gaze again, so earnest, full of regret an longing. "Whenever the hat touched my head, I couldn't stand still. I had to walk, and after finding myself outside the village and far down the road several times, I wrapped it up in a cloth and buried it in the yard." His lips quivered. "I was married. I couldn't leave Marta, not because a magical hat told me I was wrong." He sighed. "It wasn't bad, not like this."

He waved his hand around the room. "Once I'd buried the hat, we were happy for many years. Dear Marta, she died in childbirth, taking my son with her."

"I'm sorry to hear that." She'd never borne a child either, a fact George threw in her face whenever she dared whisper a complaint about his evening absences.

He took a deep breath. "Alone again, I dug up the hat. The moment I put it on, I started walking. It had this pull to it, drawing me to you. Sadly, a man can't live just by walking. He needs to eat and drink and perhaps buy a new shirt and shoes now and then. Wouldn't do to show up on your doorstep as a naked beggar, now would it?" He winked.

She caught a giggle behind her hand.

"As the hat led me from province to province, village to city, to field and forest, I had to find work from time to time. I've been traveling for years, and when I finally came to this city's gates, I knew I'd found you."

"How?"

Eddie thumped his chest. "I felt it."

She swallowed hard, heart racing. Was this what magic felt like? Was it the same thing he'd felt? "May I touch it? The hat?"

He looked at the hat in his lap, running his hands over it. After a moment, he nodded, holding the hat out over the plate of cakes.

Her fingers brushed the brim. A jolt ran through her hand, up her arm and throughout her entire body in a single second.

Eddie gasped. His wide eyes met hers. "You felt that too?"

She nodded, so giddy she didn't trust herself to speak. That was definitely magic at work. It was real.

And if the spell on his hat was real, maybe what

she'd felt when making that long ago birthday wish had been, too.

He stared at the hat in his hand, and then finally set it down on the table, appearing utterly at ease even though it was no longer in his grasp. "I had to work for a while, earn enough to be presentable here. Your servant wouldn't have let me through the door otherwise. All the while, I'd been hoping to catch you out of the house. Would have saved us some time."

"I'm not allowed out of the house."

"It's a shame for a man to keep such beauty all for himself."

A giggle escaped her lips, and this time, she made no effort to hide it in spite of his foolish words. The mirror on her dressing table reminded her of her greying hair and sagging skin every morning.

"You're too kind. I may have been beautiful once, but that was long ago."

"I beg to differ."

Heat rushed over her face.

Clyde loudly cleared his throat. No doubt he would report all of this to George whenever he finally deemed it time to come home. She struggled to compose herself.

Eddie glanced at Clyde and then her for a long moment. She should tell him to leave, for both their sakes, but she didn't want to. "But you found me here."

He nodded. "After watching your house for weeks, it became clear that you never left it. I've watched your husband too, seeing where he goes and what he does before he comes home."

She knew well enough what he did when he was working late. One didn't come home smelling of wine and women from reading letters or meeting with citizens. She looked at the darkening sky.

"He's at the inn, with a blonde on..."

She held up her hand, shaking her head. She should be mad, fuming even, but tonight, for once, she wasn't. Tears came to her eyes, thinking of all the years she'd wasted within these walls.

"Ma'am, this has gone on quite long enough." Clyde inserted himself into their conversation. He approached Eddie. "You've upset the lady. I'm going to have to ask you to leave."

Eddie stood. "I will not leave without Juliet." He looked at her. "Unless she wants me to go?"

"I most certainly do not." She rose to her feet. "I've been upset for far too long. I'm tired of it. I'm done."

Clyde turned to her and scowled. "Ma'am, I will be relaying this conversation in its entirety to your husband."

Faint stars twinkled in the dimming sky. She took a deep breath and lifted her chin high. "Be sure not to leave anything out."

Eddie picked up his hat in one hand and held out the other. "Juliet?"

She took his hand firmly in her own. They marched past Clyde.

"I'm glad I finally found you," he said.

"I'm glad you did too, even though you took an awfully long time about it."

He squeezed her hand and grinned. "I promise I'll make it up to you."

"I see why they call you Charming Eddie."

Placing the red hat on his head, he led her out of the house and into the night air and they lived happily ever after.

HEALER

Jillian breathed deep through her nose and focused on the young man on the hospital bed beside her. His breathing remained troubled even after the two-hour healing session she'd just performed. Doctors and nurses hovered in the hallway, poking their heads in to check on her progress from time to time. The pleading eyes of his wife on the other side of the bed and the photo of their two children on the bedside table wouldn't allow her to give up.

She took a few moments to focus on the room, giving her body time to regroup. The remaining session would drain her, but she was so close with Mike that she didn't dare stop now.

He needed her. Someone always did. The patients on her list would have to wait another day.

The television was silent but photos of missing children flashed by behind the program host. She secretly wished someone would steal her away. To be free of obligation, guilt and constant fatigue... Jillian sighed.

She again rested her hand on her patient's cool, clammy arm, reforming the lifeline that linked them together. Jillian summoned the gift within her.

A tingle rose in her chest, building, and then flowing upward into her shoulders. It shot down her left arm and swelled in her hand. There the tingle coalesced until it gathered heat.

Jillian let go of her body, knowing it would sit there in the chair as if she were asleep, waiting for her return. Her awareness seeped through the palm of her hand and into the arm of the man on the bed. His heartbeat became hers as she traveled along his arm, winding, twisting her way toward his chest. The heartbeat grew louder, accompanied by the droning of rushing blood.

Somewhere in the room, people were talking-- probably the attending doctor checking in again. The sound reminded her of when she was younger, listening to her mother chat with her friends in distant, muffled voices while Jillian and the other children played tag underwater in the neighbor's pool. Those pleasant, lazy days were long gone.

She spread herself through the body, seeking out the black shadows of illness and burning them away with her heat. With all sign of the shadows vanquished elsewhere, she focused on the stubborn ones in the body's lungs.

She knew she was making progress because the body now insisted that its name was Mike. He hadn't been aware enough the last few times to put up an internal fight. Now he attempted to push her away.

She pressed her thoughts on his defensive force. "I'm trying to help."

Sometimes bodies were receptive to her presence, talking with her and allowing her control of their muscles and functions when she needed it. But most men didn't seem to like her female presence. Perhaps it was too foreign to them.

Mike fought, using his precious energy to oppose her rather than rest. Muscles bunched up, squeezing and shifting, escaping her calming control and dividing her focus.

Jillian didn't want to find out what would happen if a patient were to die while they were both entangled in a healing trance. Would she die when her lifeline collapsed, or become a passenger stuck in someone else's body? If he became too aggravated, she'd have to abort her mission or risk finding out.

The shadows taunted her, dark and boiling with malignant energy. These were the times Jillian wished she had a weapon other than willpower and heat. But swords or handguns couldn't follow her into a patient's body and medicine had failed. This was a war she had to fight alone.

Jillian gathered her being into a cloud that rivaled the size and mass of the shadows. The tingle's energy crackled within her. Heat pulsated, growing and glowing a deep red at the edges of her hazy vision.

For a moment she swore she saw white eyes glaring at her from within the shadows. Then they were gone, and like the other times her imagination had played the same trick on her, a chill ran through her being, disrupting her focus.

The shadows formed a wall. The line of war had been established.

Jillian let her heat build until her exit path began to tremble. If she let go of the path, she'd have no way back to her own body. She considered calling off her efforts for the day and coming back tomorrow recharged, but the thought of Mike dying while she rested peacefully goaded her onward.

The healing heat rose until she could hold it no longer. She hurled it at the shadows. They absorbed the heat and extinguished the faint nebulous glow.

Shaking with exhaustion, Jillian backed away. Instead of growing and coming after her as she feared, the shadows began to pulse. They lost a shade of black, fading to deep grey. Then they grew lighter and lighter until they dissipated entirely.

Relief washed over her as she drifted away. Unable to muster any energy of her own, she let the faint lifeline return her to her own body.

Jillian gasped as her awareness synced with the breathing of her own lungs and beating of her own heart. Her eyes squeezed shut against the bright hospital lights. She dropped her head into her hands and wished nothing more than to be in her bed at the hotel across the street.

"You did it! Just look at him, he looks better already," an exuberant voice informed her. Arms wrapped around Jillian's shoulders and squeezed her tightly. "I can't thank you enough."

"It's okay, really." Jillian resisted the urge to push Mike's wife away. She needed space. She needed sleep.

Mike's wife clutched his limp hand while beaming at her as if she'd just performed a miracle. "Your gift is precious. Don't pay any attention to those doubters. People can't just jump up from terminal cancer and go about their lives as if they'd suffered nothing more than a mild headache. True healing takes time. You make that time possible."

She reached out and took Jillian's hand, forming a chain between the three of them. "I would be happy to stand by your side and tell the world how wrong they are."

"That's not necessary." Jillian mustered a weak smile. "I just want to help where I can, and remember, you signed the contract."

"I know, but you could help so many more people if they truly understood."

Jillian slipped her hand from the woman's loose grasp. "This hospital, these doctors, they support me well enough. I'm not looking for fame."

She was only one person and she could only do so much. Her energy wasn't infinite. People wouldn't understand that any more than the fact that she could aid in healing, but not offer instant recovery. She'd had enough of the public ridicule and reading dueling

117

stacks of hate mail and desperate pleas for her help. That's why she was here, hiding behind a wall of confidentiality contracts in a hotel.

Doctor Kellar entered the room and went directly to Mike's side. He checked Mike's breathing and his pulse. He turned to smile at Jillian. "We'll have to run tests, of course, but from what I can see here, his condition has vastly improved. Thank you, Ms. Baare."

Jillian nodded.

"Would you like someone to bring you to your room?"

"That would be wonderful, thank you." As tired as she was, the walk to her hotel room across the street seemed like a trip to another country.

Doctor Kellar left, and moments later, an attendant came in, pushing a wheelchair. He wheeled it next to where Jillian sat. "Do you need help?"

She shook her head. Her hands and arms shook when she grabbed the arms of the wheelchair and swung herself into it. Her behind dropped into the seat with an unceremonious thump.

Mike's wife hovered over him, still holding his hand and grinning from ear to ear as tears slipped down her cheeks. She met Jillian's gaze. "Thank you. I wish there was more I could say."

"I wish there was more I could do."

"I wouldn't ask it of you even if you could. You're exhausted. Go, rest." She offered her benediction with a smile and shooing motion.

Jillian nodded to the attendant, who pushed her

out of the room and down the hall to the elevator. "You did a good thing in there," he said.

"Thanks."

They always had kind words for her after the fact. It was the begging and pleading beforehand that rubbed her nerves raw. Then again, after a healing session, her nerves were raw too. Couldn't she just teleport to her room so she didn't have to talk to anyone else? That would be a handy gift to have.

Jillian realized the attendant wasn't heading for the hotel. "Where are we going?"

"Cafeteria. You made me promise to bring you there before we returned to the hotel last time I helped you. You told me not to take no for an answer because you needed to eat. Excuse me for saying so, but you look three times worse today. You're going to eat something."

She couldn't help but smile. The staff did take good care of her despite the fact that she tended to attract unwelcome attention from reporters and naysayers no matter how many aliases she used or how low a profile she kept. "Thank you."

After managing to devour a ham and cheese sandwich without ever really tasting a bite of it, Jillian sat back. The attendant resumed their trip back to the hotel.

With her stomach full, the bright overhead lights blinked on and off as her eyes sagged. Waking glimpses of white hallways lined with multicolored stripes informed her that she was nearly to the tunnel that went under the busy street between the hospital and the hotel. The whirring of the wheels changed tones as they entered the tunnel, echoing off the tile walls. A mother scolded a child in the distance. A conversation about an ailing grandmother and who was covering the insurance deductible grew in volume and then faded away. She pried her head off her shoulder when her chair came to a halt.

"Ms. Baare can't be bothered right now. No. She doesn't do interviews. Please excuse us."

The chair set off with the rhythmic steps of the attendant again lulling her to sleep. The ding of the elevator brought her around again. Within seconds, the attendant delivered Jillian to her door.

A woman in scrubs approached them. "I'll take her from here."

"I'll be fine," said Jillian.

"Oh nonsense. You're tired. It's plain to see. You work so hard here, let me help you." The woman waved the attendant away.

Jillian fumbled in her pants pocket for the keycard. The woman took it from her and slid it through the lock. The door clicked.

"There now. Let's get you inside and into bed." She rolled the chair into the room.

Jillian tried to see the name on the ID card hanging around the woman's neck. Usually using their names got made them feel acknowledged and they'd leave her be. She kept moving, adjusting the chair alongside the bed and then helping Jillian to her feet. She gave up trying to be polite and snapped, "I'm fine now, really."

The woman left her side and went to the door. The lights went out. The lock clicked. Jillian let herself relax and sank back onto the bed.

Just as she was drifting off to sleep, the door opened. "Who's there?"

"Stay where you are."

The lights came on. Jillian blinked. The woman stood there with a young child in her arms. She rushed to the bed and place the girl next to Jillian. Then she pulled a gun from the back of her waistband.

Sweat broke out on Jillian's brow and her hands grew clammy.

"Heal her."

She'd seen many horrible diseases in her years as a healer, but none of them struck her as deeply as the sight of the bloody two-year-old in a yellow sundress with a bullet hole in her abdomen.

"I can't."

"Don't lie to me. That man confirmed who you were in the tunnel. I know you can. Maybe you just don't want to." She leveled the gun at Jillian. "How about now?"

"I'm sorry." She looked down on the pale face of the little girl and felt within herself, checking her energy. It wasn't enough. She'd drained too much on Mike. It would be another full day before she was ready to face her waiting list. "Bring her across the street. The doctors can fix her."

"No. I can't. You do it."

"Why would you wait here for me? There's a

hospital right there. What kind of mother are you?"

"You don't understand." The woman's shrill voice rose to a wail. "If you don't save her she'll die. My baby will die."

"Keep your voice down." The last thing she needed was more attention, for the media to grab onto a story, drag her through the mud again and bring a host of desperate people to her door. She'd have to find a new hospital to work with. A whole new raft of agreements and contracts floated before her eyes, blurring the view of the girl bleeding on her bed.

The mother waved the gun at her, moving closer. "I don't care what it costs. You will heal my daughter. Now."

"Please, put that away. I'll do what I can for her. You'll have to take her to the hospital as soon as I'm done. I won't be able to do more than stabilize her."

"I can't go to the hospital."

"Of course you can. If you don't have money, they'll work with you. They're not heartless."

"They'll find out. They'll take Emily from me. I can't let them do that. I can't."

Jillian ignored the woman's ranting and sunk deep into herself. The only way to get the gun out of her face and help Emily was to travel into her.

She melted inward, leaving Emily's mother behind. The room dimmed and her vision took on a red tinge. The familiar tingle within grew, swelling until it pushed her into the little girl's body.

Emily's pulse was faint. The shadows had a firm

hold on her young body. Pitch black clouds surrounded the bullet hole. Greyness pulsated everywhere she looked.

There was so much to fix, so many shadows. Jillian faltered.

The distant muffled voice of the woman rose higher. Jillian began to wonder about the safety of the body she'd left behind. Would the woman shoot her, thinking she'd fainted? She'd had no time to explain the process.

Determined to at least make an honest effort, Jillian concentrated her heat on the vital organs. The shadows surrounding the girl's heart ebbed.

Jillian pulled back into her own body. Her voice trembled with exhaustion. "I've done all I can. You need to get her to the hospital now."

"I won't let them take my baby away." Emily's mother leveled her gun at Jillian.

She held up her hands as if skin and bone could shield her from a bullet. "I wish I could do more. I'm very sorry, but I really need to rest now."

"No."

"Lady, you won't have a baby to lose if you don't get her to the hospital immediately."

"I'll kill you if you don't heal her."

"A lot of good that will do. Your daughter and I will both be dead."

"I don't have much choice. You know my secret."

"Look, whatever your secret is, you know mine too. Please, your daughter will die if you don't go."

"They'll find out she isn't mine." The woman fired the gun.

Jillian's heart forgot how to beat. She screamed. The room dimmed and then got brighter again. Bile rose in her throat. Then she realized she wasn't hurt, though she still had the urge to throw up.

"Are you insane?"

"Don't call me that!" The woman took aim, clearly not meaning to miss this time. "Help her!"

Jillian drew a deep breath and gathered her scattered nerves. She sunk back into her healing trance, centering her awareness and seeping back into Emily.

The little girl had already slipped backward during the time Jillian had been gone. She didn't have the strength to overpower the armed woman or to carry Emily to the hospital herself. She could only hope she had the strength to face the shadows again and that the woman would see reason this time. She gathered her heat and battled the shadows.

Emily's eyelids fluttered.

"Can you hear me, baby?" Mona cradled the bloody little girl in her arms.

Emily's blue-green eyes opened. Tears welled in them and spilled down her round cheeks. "Mommy?"

"Yes, baby. You're going to be okay now." She hugged the little girl to her chest.

Emily clung to her, chubby little fingers digging

into her shoulders. Mona didn't mind at all. She rubbed her cheek against the baby-soft one, reveling in the warmth she again felt there.

"Do you hurt anywhere?"

"No. Sleepy."

"Okay. Let's get you out of that dirty dress and find some pajamas. Then you can take a little nap." Mona kissed Emily's forehead. She held the little girl tight as she stood.

The healer lay still on the bed. Mona nudged the woman with her knee. Nothing. At least she'd healed Emily before passing out.

Mona went into the bedroom. Ms. Baare had to have something Emily could use. She couldn't very well carry her around in bloody clothes. People would ask questions and questions could attract the police.

She set Emily on the bed and undressed her. A warm washcloth from the bathroom helped to remove the bloody nightmare from Emily's skin. Two more finished the job. Mona threw the soiled washcloths in the corner. She didn't want any reminders of the drive-by shooting that had nearly taken Emily from her. They'd never go to a playground near a busy street again. Or any playground. The image of Emily falling from the swing right in front of her, bloodied and bawling would be forever etched in her memory.

Thanks to the healer, Emily was whole and healthy and still with her. Nothing could change that now.

Mona rooted through the drawers and found a white t-shirt. She slipped it over Emily's head. "There you go, baby. You look just like a little angel." She ran her fingers through Emily's blonde curls. With Emily in her arms, she went back to the living room.

Emily twisted in her grasp. "Who that?"

"Nobody, baby. She's just taking a nap. Shall we go home now?"

Emily stared at the woman on the floor. "Down."

"No. We need to go home now."

"Down," Emily insisted.

Mona sighed. The nagging feeling in the back of her mind told her that she needed to check the woman anyway. She couldn't very well leave the healer alive to talk to the police. All the damned missing child posters in the post offices and supermarkets were bad enough.

She knelt down and put her hand on the still woman's lips. Nothing. Not even the faintest hint of breath. She smiled.

Emily touched the face of the healer, stroking her cheek. "Night night."

With the little girl seemingly satisfied, Mona grabbed Emily and left. The police could make what they wanted from the bloody scene. Maybe they'd think there had been an attack. She didn't have time to waste finding the single bullet she'd fired, but the gun wasn't hers anyway. She'd bought it from some guy on the street three days ago and who knew where he'd got it from.

"What do you think about being Canadian, honey?"

Emily had already closed her eyes. Her sure and steady breathing brought warmth to Mona's heart. No one would recognize them there. All they had to do was make it across the border.

No one stopped them as they left the hotel. Mona hummed a lullaby she remembered hearing someone sing to a baby in a movie. Lilacs scented the air as she traveled down the sidewalk. Sunlight warmed her skin.

The rusted, silver sedan sat in the parking space alongside the park right where she'd left it. She couldn't bear to look at the park or the swings. The park should have been a safe place, and this one mostly vacant, had set her at ease, no meddlesome people on cell phones that she had to worry about calling the police. Now she knew the true reason why no one played there.

A car drove by slowly. Her heart pounded. She couldn't remember what the other one had looked like before the bullets flew. This one kept going.

Her hands shook as she quickly buckled Emily into the stolen booster seat. Another car turned the corner and headed towards her. She ran around her car and got in, thrusting the keys into the ignition. The engine rumbled to life. She fumbled with the radio knob, hoping to check for news reports, but it seemed to be on one of it's not working whims. She gave up on it and headed to the nearest northbound highway. Emily's head was already resting on her shoulder, eyes closed before she got up the ramp.

Ohio had given way to Michigan before she heard Emily stirring around in the back seat. "Waking up, baby? Do you need to go to the bathroom?" Potty training on the run wasn't the easiest thing, but when she'd taken Emily three months ago, she'd been in underwear, so she thought she'd better keep up the effort. Besides, she didn't have money for diapers.

"I gotta go." Emily squirmed in her seat.

"We'll stop in just a minute. I need to get gas anyway." Mona pulled into the next gas station. After she'd parked the car, she unbuckled Emily.

The little girl pushed her away. "I do."

"Sure, baby, you can get out by yourself."

Emily didn't want her help in the bathroom either. She closed the door to the stall before Mona could get in. The lock clicked.

"Let mommy in. You need help. That's a big toilet."

"No."

"Emily. Really. Let me in. This isn't funny. You could get hurt."

"I do."

Mona bit her lip. This was the first time Emily had refused her help. Ever since she'd stopped crying for her other mommy and accepted Mona, she'd been very cuddly. It was almost as if she was afraid to let Mona out of her sight.

"What's gotten into you?" Was this the terrible twos she'd heard so much about? As terrible as they might be, as long as she had her baby, it didn't matter. She'd love her right through two and three and everything afterward.

The toilet flushed and the door opened. Emily walked out, her bare feet padding over the gray painted cement floor.

"You did that all by yourself?"

"Yep. I big girl."

It suddenly seemed so. Mona wasn't sure what to make of this new advancement. She liked the needy toddler better. Having someone need her made the nights warmer and her days brighter. Someone had to listen to her for a change. That felt pretty good.

"Are you hungry, honey?"

"I wash hands first."

Since when did two-year-olds care about washing their hands? They ate old gum from under tables if you didn't watch them.

"I'll help you. You can't reach." She scooped Emily up and held her next to the rust-stained sink. The water dribbled out of the faucet. The soap dispenser was empty.

Emily's petite face crumpled up as if she were disgusted. "Icky!"

"You play in the dirt and mud puddles and you call this icky? Silly girl." Mona shook her head and carried the little girl into the gas station. She had to set her down to grab two sandwiches and two sodas but kept the little girl close as she approached the counter. "I need gas too," she told the attendant.

"Give me fifty bucks worth." She ruffled Emily's curls. "We'll eat in the car."

"Don't want to go."

Mona picked up the little girl. "That's enough, baby." She smiled at the young man and slid the cash across the counter. "Someone is grumpy today."

Emily lunged forward, grabbing the counter. "Not my mommy."

The cashier gave Mona a questioning glance as he handed her the change.

"She's two."

The cashier nodded as if that answered everything. "It will be a long year."

Mona held Emily tight and balanced the food and drinks in her other arm and hand. The walk back to the car was a precarious one. She set the drinks on top of the car and buckled Emily back in her seat.

"What's gotten into you, baby?"

Emily sulked in her seat, not even looking at her.

Mona sighed. She put their lunch in the front seat, the drinks in the cupholders, and went to pump the gas. One woman parked at the pump beside her but she didn't leave the car and she kept her purse on her arm the whole time. Hopefully, there would be other opportunities for easy money in the near future or they'd be going hungry real soon.

After squeezing out the last drop of gas, she went back around to her door only to find it locked. Emily stood on the front seat, showing off her pearl white teeth and the tiny dimple on her left cheek. Mona swore. Apparently, she couldn't take her eyes off Emily for even a minute.

"Baby, open the door."

"No."

"Emily, please." Mona looked around, but no one paid her any attention. "This isn't funny. Open the door for mommy."

"Not my mommy."

Mona laughed weakly, plastering a smile on her face. "Don't say silly things like that, baby. Open the door."

Emily crossed her arms over her chest and giggled.

"This isn't a game. Open the damn door."

"Ma'am?" the man at the pump in front of her called out. "The kid didn't touch the passenger side door. Try that."

"Thanks." Mona flashed him her best frazzled-mother smile and darted to the other side of the car before Emily caught on and continued her game. The handle creaked as she swung the door open.

She slid inside and grabbed the troublesome little girl. "That was very naughty, Emily. Mommy should spank you."

"Spank Mommy. Spank Mommy," Emily chanted. "Naughty Mommy."

"I'm not the naughty one, little miss. Now sit back in your seat and eat your lunch. If you stay put, I won't buckle you in until we get back on the road." Mona pulled the car away from the pump and into one of the vacant parking spaces. As she took a bite of her sandwich, she glanced in the rearview mirror.

"How on earth did you get out of your seat?" Maybe I didn't push the belt latch down all the way, she thought. The stupid thing stuck half the time. It didn't surprise her that it might have jammed and not fastened completely.

Emily nibbled at her sandwich, eating neatly for a two-year-old. "All done," she announced as she held out the empty can and wrapper to Mona.

"Thank you." Mona took the garbage and crumpled it up with her own. Making sure to keep the door open and one hand on it, she tossed the garbage into the can on the sidewalk and fastened Emily into her seat again. This time she made sure to click it closed and double checked it.

"Can't have you wandering around inside the car while I'm driving." She landed a kiss on the little girl's nose and then got back in her own seat.

Mona continued northward for an hour before jutting east. With all the people in Detroit, it would be easy to get lost in the crowd heading into Canada.

Emily squirmed in her seat. "Out."

"Sorry, baby. Gotta stay safe in your seat. I don't ever want you to get hurt again."

"No more heal. I free."

Mona's breath caught in her throat. "What did you say?"

"Out!" Emily yanked in the lap bar of her seat.

"No, before that." Mona eyed the girl in the rear view mirror.

Emily stared back. Her young, round face was innocent but her eyes were anything but.

Mona's hands shook on the steering wheel. Her voice came out even shakier than her hands. "We'll get out and play soon."

She tore her gaze from the child in the backseat just in time to see the semi stopped in front of her. "Damn traffic jams," she said as she stomped on the brake pedal. A scream welled in her throat as she realized she was too close. It was too late. The front of her car crumpled under the back end of the trailer.

The steering wheel slammed into her chest. The impact knocked the air from her lungs. The car came to an abrupt stop with an explosion of metal.

Mona coughed and drew a ragged breath. She glanced up for the rearview mirror, but the windshield's shattered glass lay sprinkled over her and what remained of the front seats. "Emily," she croaked.

The click of a seatbelt being unfastened was the only indication that Emily was alive. Seconds later, the rear door opened.

Mona tried to turn to look behind her, but pain kept her head pinned against the headrest. "Emily?"

Movement outside the car caught her attention. Mona's vision blurred as she tried to make out who stood outside her broken window. "Help," she breathed.

Emily came into focus. She stood safe and healthy on the gravel roadside. Breathing was so hard. Why was it so hard? Mona looked down. So much blood.

The little girl peered over the jagged glass at the

bent edges of the window frame. Her words were slow and deliberate. "Sorry lady, you can't heal death."

THE SPELL

Ambrose looked down at the wailing baby on the wooden floor. This wasn't good. No sir, not good at all.

"Quiet. Crying isn't going to help anyone."

The infant kicked and waved its arms about until it worked its way out of the giant robe. Then it soiled itself.

"Great, just great." Ambrose wrung his hands and paced around the chamber. "I didn't sign up to be a nursemaid, you know."

No help for that now. He sighed and wrapped the infant in the robe. "Guess we better get you cleaned up. Maybe you'll smell better once we're done."

He walked outside to the well and drew up a

bucket of fresh water. Then he dunked his screaming charge into it. The baby's face turned red with his boisterous protests. Once he was clean, Ambrose discarded the nasty old smelly robe in the garbage heap and went back inside.

Inside the big bedchamber, he rifled through trunks until he found a fine, white linen shirt. It wouldn't fit him, but, wrapped up a few times, it would do well enough for the baby.

Wrapped securely in the shirt, the baby calmed down. "See now, Simon, that's not so bad, is it?" He pondered the baby in his arms. "You're going to have to make do with goat's milk. I'm not about to get one of those nattering wet nurses from the village. We don't need anyone around here asking questions."

He fashioned a nice bed of furs in one of the large baskets he used to carry supplies up to the tower from the village. That would do well enough to contain Simon while he went out to the field to hunt down a goat and gather some milk.

When he returned, he found Simon fast asleep. He was quite a handsome baby, smooth, pale skin, round cheeks, and a fine head of dark hair. He'd be quite a favorite with the ladies once he grew up.

Ambrose set the milk aside and went back to the chamber. The book still lay open to the page he'd been using to practice his reading before Simon had surprised him. He'd been learning slowly, too slowly for his master, but with his secret practice outside their lessons, he was proud of his progress. Once he got the recitation down, he'd make a tolerable apprentice. The master said so, said he had the touch deep inside.

Ambrose's hand shook as he picked up the book. He should have listened to the words rather than practicing speaking them. He should have heard the old wizard had walked in the room. After all, the way the old man jabbed the cane into the floorboards with each shuffling step was far from quiet, but he'd been concentrating on the words.

Maybe he could find a spell to change him back. Ambrose carried the book back into the bedchamber and set the basket on the floor next to the large bed. He sat down on the thick mattress. This was way better than his cot in the kitchen.

He turned the pages, skimming the words, but after a few pages, he realized he wasn't reading them. If he did manage to turn Simon back, he'd be angry. Really angry. Angry to the degree of calling down lightning to fry him up like bacon.

Maybe this wasn't so bad. Sure he'd be stuck with a baby for a few years, but was that worse than serving a demanding old man? Seemed much the same, the more he thought about it. And if Simon eventually remembered what Ambrose had done, he'd have his youth back. Seemed a fair trade-off for missing a few years of his life. At least his anger might not get to the lightening stage.

Ambrose closed the book and spread out on the bed. Tonight he'd enjoy a good sleep on Simon's bed. Tomorrow he'd see about making sure Simon had the happiest childhood ever.

KICK THE CAT

Shireen's cat had been a pain in the neck since I'd moved in but, now, it had literally become a pain in my neck. Having a sorceress for a girlfriend was both exciting and a little unnerving, but her legs and her lips and... Let's just say they outweighed the unnerving part. Except for the cat. The damn thing yowled whenever I got near Shireen. It hissed and attacked my feet every time I took my shoes off. It watched us in bed.

Whenever I'd complain about the cat, she'd wave it off, but it would sneak back. Biting, hissing, watching. She'd tell me to ignore it.

One night, I couldn't ignore it anymore. I kicked the little bastard in the ribs and sent it flying across the room. The next thing I know, she's fused the cat to my neck. Seriously. Right to my damned neck.

Now, this might be a somewhat welcome turn of events if it were the dead of winter, but being mid-summer, I'm sweating enough already. I don't need an angry furball scarf. His claws dig into my shoulders. I'm bleeding all down my chest and back.

His tail keeps flicking into my eyes. You know how annoying an eyelash is in your eye? Try cat fur. Lots of cat fur. I've never been allergic to cats, but I think I am now. Probably did that too. Damn her.

My eyes have swollen up and turned red. I keep sneezing, and that does nothing in my favor because every sinus-racking sneeze scares the cat, making it writhe, and claw, and loudly express its dislike of this situation directly into my right ear. I'm pretty sure I'm going deaf in that ear, too.

Her words on this predicament? "You need to learn to get along. Both of you." She'd glared at the cat as much as at me, and then left. Not just left the room but left the house.

I can't go outside like this. There isn't a hood big enough to hide a cat, let alone a very pissed off cat.

Eating is all but impossible. The cat kept taking bites of my food or batting the fork out of my hand, and once, managed to rake its paw across my nose and most of my cheek. I don't know what that cat had on its claws, but now the side of my face is hot and the cuts are all swollen and red.

I tried looking at my back in the mirror, but the cat got all sorts of angry when it saw its reflection. I ended up with a hundred more gouges for my trouble.

Three miserable days later, Shireen came back.

The cat let out a pitiful meow that reverberated through its stomach and down my neck where we were joined.

She stood there, looking beautiful as ever, hands on her black leather mini-skirt clad hips, perfectly arched brows raised. "So, you've both learned your lesson?"

"Yes," I said. "You're insane. Get this damned thing off me."

The cat beat my head with its paws, claws fully extended, ripping hair from my scalp.

She sighed and shook her head. "Very well." She waved her hands in the air, making rhythmic motions and muttering under her breath.

The cat went still. Finally. Then it's weight was gone.

A warm breeze blew against my skin. My spine tingled and goose bumps rose all over my body. Though she stood across the room, her touch ran over my back. I spun around to make sure someone else wasn't standing behind me.

No one was there but the cat, staring at the floor, its head hung low. What the hell was its problem? We were finally free of each other.

A roaring heat seared through me and the room shifted, blurring, fading in and out. Sure I was about to pass out, I dropped to my knees. But my knees were no longer my knees, they were feet. I caught myself with my hands before my face hit the tiled floor.

When my head stopped spinning so badly, I stood, but my eyes were still far too close to the floor for that to be right. I blinked several times.

A low voice beside me said, "It will take some getting used to."

I turned to see the cat looking at me. In the eye. Face to face.

I lifted a paw. My paw. Holy hell.

"Name's Hank," the other cat said.

My voice was odd, shaking, not my own, and the words I heard in my head didn't correspond with the sounds in my ears. "John."

He gave me that same dry look of disdain that he'd used since I'd moved in two months ago. "Yeah, I know."

"So..." A heavy emptiness built up in my stomach until I thought I might burst. "You were human too?"

"I tried to warn you, did everything I could to get you to leave."

My furry rump hit the floor as I sat down, tail wrapped around my legs like a comforting hug. "I thought you just didn't like me."

"I don't. She's mine."

Shireen sat on the couch and picked up her

phone. She dialed and patted the cushion beside her.

Hank took one look at me and trotted off. He leapt up and curled into a ball next to her, his head resting on her thigh. She stroked his head, swirling her fingers through the fur all down his back and back up again. His round eyes became contented slits. I could hear him purring from across the room.

"Hey, James. It's Shireen. Turns out I am free tonight after all. Would you like to come over?"

The hair on my back stood up. Oh hell no. She was not going to get away with this. I let out a yowl loud enough to make an alley tom proud and leapt into her lap, claws extended.

The rear set sank into Hank. He hissed and flipped onto his back, attacking me with his own claws. The front set snagged in Shireen's blouse.

She shrieked and jumped to her feet. As she tried to pry me off, the phone slipped from her hands and fell to the floor with the satisfying crack of broken glass.

Hank went flying. Bastard probably landed on his feet, but I didn't have time to find out.

Shireen started chanting again. My skin grew hot under my fur. I twisted, kicking at her with all my might, and managed to wrench myself free from her shirt just as the room started to shift again.

I didn't wait to see how tall I was or what I looked like, I just ran as fast as my four legs would go. That pace slowed considerably as my legs became even shorter and my feet smaller. My nose was suddenly perched at the end of a snout that sprouted long whiskers.

High above me, Shireen said, "I give up. He's all yours."

Hank's paws pounded the floor. Mine skittered. This wasn't a fair fight at all.

Then I saw it. A narrow shaft of light, a cracked corner in the rubber seal under the front door.

Hank was close, his cat scent made my nose twitch and my heart race. I was too out of breath to squeak in terror. I ran, darting left and right. A paw slammed down beside my haunches.

The light. I had to reach it.

"Get him," Shireen shrieked.

Hank's paw pinned the tip of my tail to the floor. I couldn't stop now. I was so close. I could smell the trees and grass. Freedom was right in front of me.

I surged forward. My tail slipped free. I squeezed through the opening, ran down the step, leapt to freedom in the overgrown lawn and landed with a thump that knocked the breath out of me.

"What's your hurry?" asked a high-pitched voice beside me.

Between pants, I managed to say, "She was trying to kill me." I turned to see another mouse standing beside me. Three more stood close by. They were all grinning.

"Congrats on making it out," said one of the others. They huddled around me. "No one wants to be the one who finally proved Hank worthy."

"You good for nothing waste of fur," Shireen

screamed. "I give you one job. I even give you help, but you can't stand that either, can you?" She huffed. "You're a cat, but you can't kill a single mouse? Not one? Worthless! I can't believe I ever married you."

Her heels stomped across the floor so loud we could hear them clearly outside. "How am I supposed to keep this place in order if you keep aggravating every man I bring home? You sucked at that job too, remember? All you wanted to do was lie around and sleep all day. So I give you a job where you can do that, and you still don't contribute to this marriage. You know what? I'm done. I can't take this anymore."

My mouth hung open. The mice all froze, gazes locked on the house.

The door opened to reveal Hank dangling by his scruff in Shireen's hand. "John was on to something I should have done long ago." She dropped him. Her pointed shoe wound up for a stunning dropkick that sent wailing Hank flying over the yard and halfway across the street.

He did not land on his feet.

She stood in the doorway, watching as he limped away. Once he was out of sight, she turned her attention to the lawn. A scowl grew on her face, then vanished into pouty lips.

Her voice turned soft. "I know some of you are still out there. I'm sorry we fought. Really, I am. He wasn't a good husband. I know that. You deserve a second chance."

She tapped her chin, slowly surveying, seeking

us out in the towering, thick blades. "I promise to return to human form the first man who comes forward to be my new husband."

The mice-men around me eyed one another. They looked me.

"You're the one. You defeated Hank. Go on."

"Hell no. I'd rather eat cheese for the rest of my life."

"We don't really eat much cheese. We mostly eat garbage."

"Even then."

They all nodded, their whiskers twitching with laughter. We left her standing there and set off through the grass and into the garage where we celebrated our freedom with stale chip crumbs and half a can of flat beer.

MOTHER

Josiah opened his eyes and screamed. The woman looming over him was not his wife.

He distinctly remembered Shelly clutching his shoulders, telling him to hang on. Her tears had splashed down onto his face. He hadn't wanted to leave her, but the pain was too great.

The bright lights above this woman's blurry face hurt his eyes. He wanted to be alone so he could get his bearings, but people he didn't know kept picking him up and talking to him in high pitched voices that hurt his ears. They fed him, bathed him and sometimes put him in a quiet dark place so he could sleep. But each time he woke, they were there.

He wanted to ask for his wife, for their son, for his parents, even the brother he hadn't seen in years, but nothing came out of his mouth right. All he could do was kick and wail. No one seemed to understand what he wanted. They merely held him tighter and talked more.

The woman, younger than his wife, her face round and hair short and dark, picked him up. The motion made his head spin and his stomach lurch. His body wouldn't cooperate when he tried to push her away so he could make a break for the door.

The man came in, shaking his head. They talked in low voices. Their words didn't make sense, but from the tone, it sounded like an argument.

He'd remembered arguing with Shelly from time to time, especially in those first months after Michael had been born, their tempers short from lack of sleep. Was Shelly okay? He had to let her know he was all right, that he was awake again and could come home soon.

Michael would be wondering where he was, too. His little shadow would be lost without him, probably driving Shelly nuts.

He would have welcomed an argument about his absence right then if he could only speak to Shelly. But the woman rubbed his back and sang softly, lulling him to sleep. Maybe Shelly would be there when he woke.

Days went by, possibly even weeks. It was hard to keep track. He was so tired all the time. It must have been the healing. His mother had always said sleep was the best medicine.

He became aware one day as he was eating, that it was a breast against his mouth rather than a spoon or a feeding tube. It certainly wasn't Shelly's breast.

This was giant and hard and spurting warm fluid into his mouth the harder he sucked. He wanted to turn away, but he was hungry and the warm fluid made him comfortable and sleepy. And soon his eyes drifted closed.

When he woke next, the man came to get him. After a few high-pitched words, he put Josiah on the floor. The ceiling was so high. He tried to reach for it, but it was like he was lost inside a skyscraper made for giants. He examined the hand he held up over his face. It was tiny and hairless, the nails clean and trimmed. This wasn't his hand.

He wailed. The man appeared and knelt down beside him. He picked Josiah up from the floor and carried him back past three bright lights on the ceiling, past the green-and-ivory striped wall to the pale blue room where his bed was. But it wasn't his bed. His bed was king-sized with a navy blue comforter that he'd argued with Shelly for. The floral monstrosity she'd wanted would have given him headaches.

Wooden slats limited his view. He kicked and screamed.

"Quiet now."

The man turned on soft music. Lights twinkled on the ceiling above the bed. Josiah paused his tirade to watch the lights. The door closed.

The lights reminded him of something. Headlights. Pain. Shelly's tears. He wanted to go home. He squeezed his eyes shut and screamed, but neither the man or woman came. His throat hurt.

Eventually, he stopped. It wasn't helping anyway. No one seemed to care that he was scared and alone.

It wasn't until weeks later that he found he could move on his own. This body he'd been stuck in wasn't his, but he could control it somewhat. The man had put him on the floor again and was sitting nearby, watching the television. Josiah focused on the long wide screen, listening to the words. He concentrated hard and they slowly started to make sense. It wasn't a program he recognized, and all the pictures were brightly colored and people wore odd clothing.

If the man was distracted, maybe he could get away. He rolled over and pulled himself up on his arms and knees. If he blocked out the television and the man, he could concentrate on making his limbs move. Josiah rocked back and forth a few times, trying to get a feel for the way his body moved. It was sluggish, all his limbs weak and plump. Where had the muscles gone that he'd spent so many hours a week working on? Then he remembered that this wasn't his body.

What was before and now swirled in his head. He whimpered, the effort of keeping it all straight was too much. Some fresh air would help. He spotted the door. It was impossibly tall, but he had to get to it. Josiah rocked back and forth until his arms shook and his legs quivered beneath him. The door opened. He would have darted toward it if his legs worked properly, but instead, he fell to his stomach on the floor, having only managed to squirm a couple feet in all that time.

The woman set her keys and purse on the table beside the door and then scooped him up. She carried him around, talking to the man. The feeling of her bare shoulder against his cheek was comforting. She smelled like sunshine. He found himself nuzzling her skin rather than thinking about the door. He couldn't remember exactly why he had wanted to get to it.

Her words became clearer as she jiggled him in her arms, relaxing his mind and body. He was safe here. She brought him into the bedroom where she cuddled with him, bathed him and then put him in fresh clothes. They settled into the chair in the corner of his room and rocked while his stomach filled with warmth and nourishment. Josiah settled in, letting sleep take him. He would get to the door another day.

When the sunlight woke him, Josiah blinked and focused on the face of the woman. She smiled and pulled him from the bed. Her voice brought him joy. Her fingers were gentle as she changed his clothes and fed him. Contented, he let her carry him through the house until she handed him over to the man.

The door closed. The man held him for a few minutes and then gently set him on the floor. The television turned on. The channels flipped by. There were so many of them. How long had he been here and where had he been before this? He couldn't remember.

He rolled around, looking for the door. When he

finally spotted it, he got to his hands and knees. Something was outside that door that he needed. A woman and a boy, but who were they? He rolled onto his back and pondered his hand and then a foot. The foot was clean and soft. That seemed wrong. But this was his foot. Why was that wrong?

Josiah slid a finger into his mouth. As his gums met the skin he knew for sure that this was his hand. It was part of him. This was his body. But it wasn't, was it?

He stared at the ceiling fan for a while, trying to sort through his memories. The fan blades spun round and round. The television droned on. Josiah found himself missing the woman who cared for him. Part of him felt guilty for that, but she'd been nothing but kind and no one else had come for him. Maybe the people he'd wanted to see so badly had forgotten about him. Had their memories gone hazy too?

The man picked him up and pried a warm nib between his lips. It wasn't skin. It didn't smell right. It wasn't the woman. He turned away, trying to escape the warm watery liquid spurting into his mouth. The man stiffened. Josiah could hear the man's heartbeat growing faster. The nib slipped between his lips again. His stomach protested the fight. He was hungry. This was food. It wasn't what he wanted, but he sucked at it anyway. At least for a little while, until his stomach was satisfied, then he spit it out. The man stood up and pressed Josiah to his shoulder, patting his back. A burp welled up within him and he let it lose. Someone would have chided him for that, but he couldn't remember who.

The man's shoulder was hard but warm. He carried Josiah to the bed in the blue room.

The woman came through the door, smiling. "Look who's awake."

Josiah tried to reach for her. She reminded him of someone. Someone he had loved. He wanted nothing more than to hold her again, but for now, he let this woman hold him instead. Someday he would be big like the man and he would take care of this woman and make her feel warm and comfortable like she did for him.

GIVING CHASE

The man behind me gasped for breath, his feet pounding the plascrete with less gusto than a block ago. "Stop, Mr. Samuels. We just want to ask you some questions."

Yeah, sure they did. I wove through the sprawling space-port market, narrowly missing a lumbering Talgasian slothlord and his scantily-clad entourage. A male grunt and female shriek informed me that the officer wasn't so lucky.

The chants of protestors drowned out the rest of the officer's shouts for my cooperation. At least he couldn't fire at me with all the people around.

I glanced over my shoulder to see him doubled over, hands braced on his thighs, and his face bright red. That one wouldn't be bothering me for a while, and we'd left his partners behind two blocks ago.

I slowed my pace to better blend with the masses who were clogging up the entire market. The crowd wanted freedom from a government bent on taking everything. This wasn't my homeworld, but I was also quite in favor of freedom at the moment.

The rendezvous point lay just ahead. I shed my bright yellow tourist shirt mid-stride, leaving me with the plain grey one I'd worn when I'd left my apartment that morning. The logo-covered shirt hadn't helped me blend as much as I'd hoped. Too many people knew my face.

One of those people was Dirk Scattergash. His deeply scarred cheeks spread into a wide grin. "Chase, I wondered if you'd make it."

"Wondered?" I snorted. "When have I not made it?" I glanced around the back corner of Dirk's favorite cheese trader's stall. Anyone who wasn't busy shopping seemed to be either watching the protestors or the reporters who had just arrived.

I ducked back behind the wall and fished the sheer bag of glowing red gems from my pants pocket. My hand shook. I clutched the bag tighter. The six-block run shouldn't have left me this exhausted. Then again, I didn't usually have four men to outrun. The damn city was crawling with security attempting to manage the outbreak and the protestors.

Dirk stared at my hand. "You're getting old."

"So are you, and you're ugly to boot."

Dirk threw his head back and laughed. "Well then, I suppose you want your payment?"

"If you want the bag."

He held out a credit chip. I held out the bag. We exchanged simultaneously as if we'd done this a hundred times before. It had probably been close to that.

"I've got another job for you."

I checked the balance on the chip. "I don't need it. This will do me for awhile." A long while really. I'd been saving up payoffs for nine months.

"This isn't about what you need."

"Cut the cryptic crap. I gotta get off this rock. The officers are everywhere and they know me."

"It's just one more job, Chase. You owe me."

I gritted my teeth. "Yeah, I owe you, but I don't plan to spend the rest of my life in a prison cell."

"Then don't get caught."

"Come on. They need to forget about me for a couple years before I work here again."

"I don't have a couple years." He dropped his hands to hover just over the lumps beneath his long open coat. I didn't know what sort of weapons Dirk carried, and I didn't want to find out.

I'd been working exclusively for him since he'd rescued my unaware ass when I'd done my first job on this planet. Turned out the crime lords didn't look fondly on freelancers. Except for Dirk. He'd negated my freelancer status by providing me with jobs and a comfortable flow of credits.

"I'm grateful for what you've done for me, really, I am, but I can't take the chance right now. Can you at least give me a couple months to get a new alias settled in?"

"The job has to happen tonight."

"That's not even enough time for research."

"I'll give you what you need to know. You just get in, get the goods and deliver them like you always do. It's what you're good at, Chase. You're the man for the job."

I'd planned on being the man enjoying a full-service hotel on a little pleasure planet somewhere, but Dirk's hands hadn't moved and he was looking less friendly by the second.

"I suppose if I say no, you have something painful in mind?"

Dirk pressed a hand to his chest. "Chase, you wound me. We're friends."

"Uh huh."

"Who gave you all those credit chips you haven't been spending?"

"That would be you."

Damn, he'd been keeping tabs on my accounts. A man who planned to stick around might have converted the chips into local currency. Chips were universal. He'd been hinting that my debt was nearly paid for months. I had a right to plan for my future.

He nodded. "You don't do this job, they'll all be empty. You won't be able to even afford passage out of this port." He stepped out into the open. "Should I just call one of those frustrated officers over? They could probably use a break after the afternoon you put them through." He started walking.

I stepped in beside him. "That's not funny."

Signs proclaiming unfair deportation of the sick and the lack of health care bobbed up and down in the chanting throng. The only officer in sight was looking the other way.

"Do I look like a comedian?"

"No."

"Damn right." He stopped to admire a blue suit that about mirrored the one he currently wore under his coat. "So are you in or are you about to be broke?"

"Not much of a choice."

"Sure there is. You could turn yourself in, plead your case about turning into an honest man, serve a good twenty years or so and enjoy the last bit of your life with a clear conscience."

"As I said, not much of a choice."

He shrugged. "Up to you."

"I'm in, dammit, but I don't like it. I do this and I'm free to leave, right?"

"Sure. You do the job, and we'll never see each other again." He handed me a quickgrade sheet with the promised information.

I studied the thin brown paper covered with neat writing. "A kid? I'm stealing a kid?"

"Is that a problem?"

"They're hard to fit in my pocket."

"Not easy to run with either, I'd imagine. You may want to rethink your exit strategy. Don't worry, you'll be compensated for the level of difficulty."

I scanned the details one more time, committing them to memory, and then activated the sheet. The paper disintegrated into dust.

"See you in the exec port bar at midnight." Dirk melted into the crowd.

I caught sight of one of the officers skulking around the nearby booths. Darting in the opposite direction, I made my way toward the single-room apartment I'd been renting. Halfway there it occurred to me that if the officers knew my name, they'd have my recent aliases as well. Maybe. They weren't always that bright. But could I take that chance? One last job and I'd be out of here. Massages by pretty women with skilled hands, cold drinks, a good smoke, maybe even not having to look over my shoulder every five minutes. All I had to do was grab a kid and my credits would be clear.

Clothes could be replaced. The book I'd been reading hadn't been that good anyway. I'd learned to travel light and keep most of my credits hidden on me in case of situations just like this one.

A quick change of direction and a two-hour walk brought me through the white stone buildings of the lower end of town to the red brick estates of the execs. I could have counted the number of trees in those two hours on one hand. Here, lush gardens filled with pungent lilies, manicured shrubs and many kinds of trees adorned the vast yards outside the estate walls. More tops of trees could be seen beyond them. The blinking lights of the exec port were visible even in the late-afternoon sky. Clean white shuttles drifted up and down like feathers on the wind, carrying passengers and cargo to and from the ships in orbit. Shortly after midnight, I'd be on one of them.

By morning the news feeds full of riots and

protests, the battle between them and us, of which I wasn't even technically part of, wouldn't matter to me in the least. All I had to do was grab a kid and deliver her to Dirk. She was one of them, these rich who drove the majority of the population into the ground. Well, her parents were, and if she stayed with them, she'd turn out no better. I'd been here long enough to see the truth of that.

Yet, the thought of kidnapping a child brought a sour taste to my mouth. This wasn't the same as snagging jewels or information. Kids were loud and had fists and feet and parents.

Could I make it off the surface before Dirk figured out that I'd run and zapped my credits? The man had connections. Even if I managed to leave, he wouldn't take my defection kindly. I wanted to live long enough to enjoy myself for a while, far from Dirk and this planet.

I ducked into a public terminal booth and booked my flight for half an hour after our midnight meeting. Maybe I should have bought that suit Dirk had been looking at so I could have fit in a little more around here. I sighed. Nothing to be done about that now. I'd have to lay low and move fast. At least Dirk would be on time and waiting. He always was.

With the address and the entry codes already in my head, all I had to do was wait. I spent a couple credits on an hour of terminal time to catch up on the local news—mostly to see if my face was posted.

Clearly, the execs were in control of the report on the protest in the marketplace. The visuals focused on dirty faces, shabby clothing of those holding the signs and shouting. They showed images of factory production lines standing still, of trash in the streets and dead bodies overflowing in the morgues. The common people were so busy protesting that they were causing their own city to fall into decay and ruin. Their own dead weren't even being processed. Those protesting were portrayed as animals.

The reporter interviewed several execs, all dressed immaculately in their fitted suits with their hair artfully slicked back from unblemished faces. They discussed plans for subduing the rebels, most of which included deadly force. One man, with strong features and a golden pin of office on his collar, looked straight into the camera.

"Anyone who is sick must be removed immediately to prevent the spread of the virus. Workers are paid fair wages. They should spend their money on quality food and their own healthcare instead of alcohol, drugs, and luxuries they obviously can't afford."

His jaw tightened and his brows lowered. "You don't see the virus plaguing us. We take care of ourselves. Now they expect us to take care of those who are financially irresponsible too?" He shook his head. "We're already offering the free shuttle service for removal of the afflicted. That is all we will give. Further protests will not be tolerated."

The report ended. I did a quick scan of the other headlines. Thankfully my face hadn't been featured. That would make boarding the port shuttle and enjoying my flight afterward easier, as long as none of the officers who'd been hot after me were patrolling the port tonight. I'd just have to keep calm and not give them a reason to look at me twice.

Not finding anything of further interest, I turned off the news and did a little research on the family I was about to rip apart.

When the same face I'd just seen on the news came up as the father of the kid I was about to nab, my heart dropped a little. It wasn't like Dirk to get wrapped up in politics. Was it? I'd not paid much attention to the who and why of my assignments. The only thing that had mattered to me was how much.

What would happen to this kid? Whoever financed this job hated her family and those like her. Would they harm her or just use her?

It didn't matter. It was just one kid. One night. One job. It was none of my business.

By the time I stepped from the booth, darkness had settled on the district. Shadows were a far better camouflage than daylight and the shirt I'd shed earlier printed with the logos of popular tourist attractions. I'd only gotten a stamp on one location. Maybe they'd have a less hideous version at my next port. I'd make a career out of visiting all the sponsors to get each logo stamped. Enjoy drinks in all the local bars, eat fancy meals, admire the girls dancing in clubs, relax in rooms at the luxury hotels—and at the end of it, earn some corny trinket for completing my shirt's mission. The reward didn't matter, it was the journey. That's what my father had always said. I was due for an enjoyable journey. That'd show my father, rest his soul, for burdening a thief with an inviting name like Chase.

Three columns of light shown up from the port, providing a reference point to guide me through the winding roads that allowed the execs their utterly private spaces. Walls and trees provided darkness to make my way to the address Dirk had provided.

The estate turned out to be a sprawling affair, much like all the others. It had a tall fence, which I climbed, cameras, which I avoided, sensors that I lightly stepped over, and an alarm-rigged back window that I deactivated and opened. Dirk's information had been very thorough.

Lights indicated the room in the front of the house was occupied. Raised male and female voices from that direction told me the parents were in an argument about finances and that he was on the losing end.

I crept up the stairs and past three doors to the girl's bedroom. With my sleeve over my hand, I entered the code on the entry pad. The door slid open. Soft beeps and hisses came from inside. Clear plastic surrounded the bed like a bubble. Dirk hadn't mentioned this.

Soft light illuminated a frail figure on the bed. She may have been five or six years old. Her sunken eyes were open and watching me.

Something was wrong with her, but her father had gone on record saying the virus was a lower district problem. For once, the barriers fracturing this society brought me a little relief.

Even so, using a sick kid against her parents was damn low. Did she need all this stuff to survive? Was I going to kill her by taking her away? Kidnapping was one thing, but murder? I stood in the doorway, watching her watching me, listening to the parents screaming at one another.

Dirk knew she was ill. He'd had too much information not to know. He'd have proper care for her. He had to. A dead kid wasn't very useful as leverage. I located the entrance to the bubble and dashed inside. Air thick with moisture and disinfectant slithered over my skin.

The girl smiled and held out her arms. I turned around, expecting her parents to be standing behind me, but we were alone.

"I'm ready," she said.

Was she part of this? Did she know I'd be coming for her? Grateful that she wasn't screaming, I scooped her up. She weighed half as much as I'd expected.

She gasped as we ducked out of the bubble and out of her room. We bounded down the stairs and into the room with the open window. After a split second to figure out how to slide out of the window with her in my arms, we were out of the house, over the sensors, under the cameras and in front of the wall.

The wall proved a bit more daunting than the window. Her thin arms clung around my neck as it was. She wasn't protesting. Maybe I was doing her a favor. If that was the case, I figured she could do her part in this escape from her bubble.

"Hang on tight. We're going over."

She tucked her head under my chin and wrapped her legs around my ribs. Up and over the wall went smooth as can be with all my limbs free. On the other side, I took stock of what Dirk wanted in his arms in half an hour.

"What's your name?"

"Shayla."

"You want to walk, Shayla?"

She shook her head. Her arms and legs trembled. Poor thing was scared.

"I'm not going to hurt you."

"You're a funny looking angel."

"I'm no angel." I started toward the port.

"Momma says angels have big feathery wings. You don't have any. Why not?"

"Wings would be handy, but I guess mine never grew in."

"That's all right." She patted my shoulder. "I'm still happy you're here. Momma said you'd come one day soon. I was very tired of being in bed and alone. She wouldn't even hold me anymore."

"Maybe you'll be happier now."

"She said I would be when I was free. Will I get wings?"

"Can't say for sure." I hoped Dirk was good to the kid. She seemed like a sweet girl.

"Have you seen Grace?"

"Who's Grace?"

"My nanny. She was one of the first ones to get sick."

Get sick? My heart dropped. "Does your nanny live by you?"

Shayla shook her head. "She lived hours away."

Dirk could not have done this to me. The words caught in my throat, "How's Grace doing?"

"She died." Tears welled in her eyes.

A tremor ran through my body. I should drop the kid and run. But run where? I was already infected.

I set Shayla down and dislodged one of my credit chips from inside the seam of my shirt. I scanned it. Empty. My legs went out from under me. I plopped down in the grass beside the road.

Shayla got to her feet and looked up and down the road. "This would be easier if you had wings. You wouldn't have to walk so far."

I nodded, barely hearing her over the racing blood throbbing in my ears. I was going to die. I swallowed hard.

"How much farther do we need to go?"

The lights of the port bar blinked brightly in the center of town. I picked her up and started walking.

Shayla's arms and legs shook worse. "I'm so tired and it hurts."

"How long have you been waiting for me?"

"A week. Momma got me good medicine. She wouldn't let Daddy ship me away to die."

I adjusted her back into my arms where she curled up against my chest like a contented kitten.

"How long did Grace hold on after she got sick?"

Shayla shrugged. "One day she was sick. She didn't come back."

I didn't have a bubble of medicated air. Neither did Shayla now. And without any credits, we weren't getting one. I glanced back at her home. Maybe I could sneak her back in. We could share the medicine. But it wasn't healing her. It was only prolonging the inevitable.

Dirk wanted us at the port bar. If he was stupid enough to meet me there, I certainly wanted the chance to breathe in his face. And if he didn't, I hoped the virus found him anyway. Bastard.

We made it to the port entrance without incident. With the kid in my arms, I supposed I didn't look like anyone out to cause trouble. No one looked twice when I walked into the port lobby and consulted the map for the location of the bar. Traffic was light given the late hour. Loud music and the stink of liquor and sweat told me I'd found the right place.

Laughter and business deals mingled with smoke and over-priced food. High heels and suits, short skirts, heavy cosmetics, leering grins and wandering hands filled the tables. The only thing that set this bar apart from the public port I'd been in earlier was the quality of the clothing, richness of the smoke and purity of the liquor. They were no better than the rest of the population. They didn't deserve all their nice things that everyone else worked so hard for. Maybe those protestors had a point after all.

We went inside but hung at the back while I scanned the crowd for Dirk.

"Why are we here?" Shayla asked.

"I gotta hand you over to my boss."

"Oh." She nodded knowingly. "Momma said it would be something like that."

Gazes began to drift in our direction. Without anywhere specific to head, I meandered around the outside row of tables, hoping to appear like I was mingling, with a kid in my arms, in a bar. I huffed into my free hand and dragged it over every table we passed. The seated occupants glared at me. I made sure to look directly at them and enunciate slowly when I said, "Have a nice night."

Still no sign of Dirk. Had he planted the sick nanny in Shayla's house? Had he wanted me to spread the virus here after his first effort had come up short? Despite not wanting to do Dirk any favors, given the circumstances, I wasn't exactly opposed doing just that.

I found an empty table and set Shayla in one of the chairs. Sweat seeped into my shirt and dripped down my forehead. Shayla's skin paled a few more shades, the shadows under her eyes darkening.

"Excuse me," said a red-lipped exec in a blouse with all but the bottommost buttons undone. "Children aren't allowed in here. "You're going to have to bring your daughter home and then come back for a good time later."

"We're waiting for someone. We won't be long."

She leaned in closer. "You need to leave now.

This isn't an appropriate place for a child."

I took her hand and kissed it. "So sorry. We will be on our way shortly."

The woman quirked a finely plucked brow. "Maybe I should get security?"

"Go right ahead." Never thought I'd be saying those words. I laughed out loud.

Shayla smiled at the woman. "You don't have any wings either."

"She will soon," I said, still laughing.

The woman pulled away. "What are you talking about?"

"Don't worry about it. Life's too short." I waved her away.

She headed toward the bar and the tall, bulky man who stood next to it.

"I'll be right back." I stood up and made my way through another section of tables. A waitress passed by. I grabbed a drink from her tray and tossed it back.

"You can't do that," she said. The man at the table she'd been about to serve got to his feet.

I put my hand on his shoulder and exhaled. "Sorry, I was thirsty."

"You owe me a drink," he said.

"Sure, let me go grab my credit chip." I wandered back to my table with him following close behind.

"What the—" he came up short when he saw Shayla. "You can't bring... She looks really sick."

"She is. Oh, and I am too." I held up a chip. "You still want that drink?"

His gaze darted around the room. He shook his head. "I gotta go."

"You should all go," I said, raising my voice above the music. "You'll want to find Dirk Scattergash. He's the one who brought the virus to you."

Heads turned to me. The flashing rainbow lights of the dance floor reflected on wide eyes and stunned faces. A woman shrieked, "You've killed us all!"

I grabbed a drink from the table next to ours and raised it. "Make sure to shake Dirk's hand for me. Name's Chase, by the way. Nice to meet you all."

The music went dead. People jumped to their feet.

The four people at the table nearest to us yelled obscenities and ran to the exit. The bouncer yelled about quarantine protocols, but no one seemed to listen. The place emptied as fast as if someone had flipped on the closing time ugly lights.

I dropped into my seat and tossed back the drink. Two more followed.

"How much does it hurt?"

"A lot, but don't worry," Shayla said, "Angels can't get sick."

"Right, I forgot about that." Even the employees and the guy who had been going on about the protocols had left. I got up and grabbed a bottle from behind the bar.

A lump formed in my throat. I coughed into my hand to clear it only to discover flecks of blood in my spittle. I'd only been with her, what, an hour?

Dirk might have left me without a credit to my name and a deadly virus, but I had a nice girl to talk to, a lot of good booze and there wasn't a soul looking at me with suspicion. I intended to enjoy every second I had left, secure in the knowledge that those I'd just infected would see to it that Dirk didn't live past morning either. There wasn't a big enough rock for him to hide under with that many execs on his tail. Screw me over? I shook my head and took a long draw from the bottle and then another.

"I was really looking forward to a massage." Warmth flowed down my throat and settled in my stomach. I fished all the credit chips out of my hidden pockets and set them on the table.

Shayla began to build a tower with them while I emptied the bottle. I helped her finish her creation, topping it off with the last chip I'd received from traitorous Dirk. She knocked it down and laughed. It was a beautiful sound. We built it again.

"Let's leave this one," she said.

It would be our memorial. A shining tower of empty chips.

I picked her up and set her back on my lap. Despite all the liquor I'd just drank, my throat was dry. My head throbbed even through the pleasant haze of intoxication and black spots edged my vision. "We might as well sit here together while we wait for the big boss, eh?"

She snuggled up against me and then landed a little peck of a kiss on my cheek. "I'd like that very much."

CHETRIC THE GRAND

Lightning flashed outside the basement window. Chet Wykowski gripped his controller, praying to the game gods that the power wouldn't go out while he was in the middle of the quest he'd been working on for the past two hours. Rain beat against the house and thunder rumbled, but the TV and game console stayed on. He relaxed into the couch, reaching out blindly for the bag of nacho chips that had been his sole source of sustenance since downloading Wizards and Warriors six hours ago. His fingers met with nothing but greasy crumbs. Wiping his hand on his pants, he reached for the can of lukewarm soda beside him and settled back into the game.

As he took yet another beating from the heavily armored Orc Lord and applied his last healing potion, he began to consider that he might need to waste more time on side quests to level up his character before trying for the Orc again. A level five wizard just wasn't cutting it. But he was sick of delivering items from one town to another or providing safe passage for hapless travelers in exchange for a rusty knife or a threadbare rug posing as a magic carpet.

The Orc battle promised enough experience to gain him several levels and enough gold to purchase the rune-covered cloak and spell book he'd seen in the last shop.

The Orc swung his tree-trunk size spiked club at Chetric the Grand again, knocking the wizard into the wooden wall of a livery across the town square. The stupid chickens that seemed to be milling around in every town scene scattered with crazed squawking. The wood shattered with a crack that came through the sound system so loud that he thought his eardrums would burst. The room around him flashed white. Chetric's body slid down the wall and landed on the ground with a pathetic grunt and a puff of dirt. Everything went black.

Chet opened his eyes, blinking away the fog of heavy sleep. He didn't remember falling asleep. Or shutting down the game. His heart raced as he fumbled around, searching for the controller to verify that he'd hit save before nodding off.

The damned controller was nowhere to be found. And no matter how much he blinked, he couldn't quite clear his aching head. In fact, his entire body ached, even worse than his doomed two-week stint on the wrestling team in high school. He hadn't liked all the aches then, and now, three years after graduating, he didn't like them even more. Grimacing, he worked his way into a sitting position.

He tried to find the can of cola to wash away the sandy grit he discovered on his teeth, but that was gone too. The sun beat down on him, making him sweat. Why was there a sun in the basement? And what the hell was this long-sleeved tunic he was wearing instead of the t-shirt and shorts he'd fallen asleep in?

Chet's eyes and mind suddenly clicked into working order.

A worn backpack lay by his side. He reached in, pulling out three turnips, a leg of mutton, and a three-page book. His eyes bulged as he read. It was the beginner spell for shooting balls of energy that worked for hobs but not much else. On the last page as a weak healing spell. Both useless.

Chickens clucked nearby. A woman in a peasant dress wandered over to him.

"Do you have a ring for me?"

"No. Go away."

"Very well. Find me later. I'll be at the Comeright Inn."

The only thing keeping Chet from losing it entirely was the fact that the Orc wasn't still there. All that remained of their battle was a broken wagon and two broken boards on the side of the building where he'd been landed after being smacked with the giant club. No wonder he ached all over.

But that meant he was in the game. Like *in* it. Chet leaned against the livery, hunched over with his hands on his knees, hyperventilating.

The sun was arcing downward before he'd gotten himself under control. If he'd somehow gotten into the game, there had to be a way out. He spotted a rusty sword in the dirt near where his backpack had been. Upon picking it up, he realized it fit in the scabbard that hung from the thick leather belt around his waist. With his backpack slung over one shoulder and the sword at his side, he ventured out into the street.

A large, grime-covered man wearing a leather apron and reeking of smoke and hot metal, took a lumbering swing at his head.

Chet dodged out of the way. "What the hell was that for?"

The big man scowled. "You're the wizard, right? You can send me home."

Revealing that his powers were not quite up to that task as of yet didn't seem wise. "I am a wizard, yes. Where is your home?"

"The north coast."

Chet did his best to recall the map in the lower corner of the screen that had slowly revealed itself during his travels. "Right. If you take this road to the left, you'll come to the port and from there you can take a ship. That's the fastest way."

"Can't you magic me there? I don't have gold for a ship."

"Sorry, no."

The blacksmith snorted. "Some wizard you are." He stormed back to his forge on the other side of the street.

Not even ten steps later, someone hit him in the back of the head with something hard. Chet put his arms up, trying to defend himself, and spun around to face his attacker.

"Send me home," cried a young boy with a long stick in his hands.

"What is it with you people?" Chet finally got out of range enough to muster his energy ball spell and send the kid flying backward.

"My uncle stole me away. He sold me." The boy got up from the dirt, tears flowing down his face. "Please, sir, you can help me?"

"Sorry, I can't." Chet hurried down the street, trying his best to avoid everyone. Sore and hungry, he sought out the inn the woman had mentioned. The more he walked around town, the more he remembered about where he'd been and where things were. Once he got his bearings, he made his way to the inn.

As he walked more footsteps followed him. He turned around to see two men, one with a large fish, the other with a game board under his arm, and a woman with a rolling pin following close behind. All three of them stopped when he caught sight of them, smiling nervously but all with the same determined gleam in their eyes. He started walking faster, the muscles in his neck and shoulders tensing further and further.

Finally, he could take it no longer. He turned around again to find a well-dressed man with a deck of cards had joined the other three stalkers. "What the are you people doing?"

The four of them looked from one to the other, shifting their feet in the dirt and pursing their lips.

The woman spoke up, "Your sign, we just want to go home."

"What sign?"

"The challenge pinned to the back of your shirt," said the man with the fish. "Beat me, and I'll send you home."

Chet tried to twist his head around to find the note. He contorted his arms to try and grab it, but his muscles were too tight. "Where?"

The man with the deck of cards approached slowly and after a tug, handed Chet a handwritten note and a pin.

"I did *not* put that there. I'm not sending any of you home or anywhere else. Now, leave me alone!" He crunched the note in his hand. That's what he got for blacking out in the middle of town. Some stupid kid had probably thought he was being funny.

Chet stormed off to the inn. No one else accosted him along the way.

Beggars sat in a row on the boardwalk outside the inn. One of which was the urchin he'd sold the threadbare rug to before he'd gone off to battle the Orc. The kid looked happy to have a rug to sit on, though the rug looked even worse for wear, now covered in mud and food crumbs.

"Looks like you're not starving then," he said to the urchin.

"No, sir. Are enjoying the stone?"

Chet had to trace back his transactions. He'd received the rug as payment for returning a doll to a girl, but then had accidentally started a riot and killed two men with his sword when his performance skill was too low. Then he'd meant to do a simple magic trick to win the favor of the miller's daughter who had promised to teach him another spell but instead had set the town's wooden granary on fire. To gain back some of his good karma, he'd traded the urchin the rug for the boy's favorite stone. The stone fit into a hole in an old woman's wall, sealing her home against the wind and earning him three turnips. He still had no idea what he was supposed to do with those.

He nodded to the urchin.

Dust puffed from beneath the boy, making the beggar next to him cough. The boy pressed his hands firmly on front corners of the rug, but the back corners continued to flap. Chet swore he heard a muffled voice, but the boy nor the man next to him said anything.

"Who is that?" He peered around.

The boy's eyes grew wide and he rocked back and forth until he was violently pitched forward, rolling head-first out into the street.

The rug rose up, standing end to end, as if it had legs. It walked forward on two corners, slapping Chet in the cheek with the third.

"You idiot," said a feminine voice. "I could have brought you anywhere you wanted to go, but you traded me for a stone? You took one look at me and thought I was worthless, didn't you?" The corner drew back as if it were going to slap him again.

Chet stepped back. "Uh, sorry?"

The rug pointed to the wad of paper in his hand. "I see you found my note."

"Yours?"

"Look at me. I mean, look at this mess!" The rug twisted side to side. "That kid hasn't had a bath in, well, ever, and his feet are covered in mud. I'm filthy."

"So..." Chet bit his lip, not sure whether to run screaming or laugh. "You want me to...beat you?"

"I thought the note was quite clear. You clean me up, trade the kid something else for me, and I'll send you home."

He removed his three turnips and set them on the boardwalk. "Those are for you, kid Sorry, I need the rug back."

Chet motioned the rug over to a grassy lot with two chickens scratching about. "Go stand over there."

The rug floated over the street and stood in the lot. Chet summoned three energy balls one after another, hitting the rug and knocking the mud and dirt away. On a whim, he threw a health spell its way too.

Color ran over the rug, bursting into intricate patterns. Long golden tassels dripped from its corners. The rug leaped into the air, laughing, rolling in tight spirals.

"You can call me Nora. Promise you won't trade me again?" it purred his ear, rubbing up against him and running a silken tassel against his cheek.

"Wouldn't dream of it, Nora."

"Then hop on then, it's time for you to go home. If you play your game right, I might even go with you."

OTHER BOOKS BY JEAN DAVIS

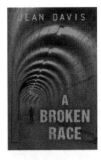

In a hard future were most of humanity are slaves to a select few, the words of a prisoner lead Joshua to the truth behind the smiles of his masters. What he does with that knowledge might save them all or doom humanity for good.

Sahmara, an escaped slave in an enemy country, prays for help, but the assistance of the gods has a price. Along with her lovers Olando and Sara, she may be the one to help take her homeland back if she can only find the strength within herself.

Abducting the angry and suicidal god of war might not be Logan's wisest choice, but she's the weapon that might be able to defeat the army of Matouk, who destroyed his homeworld. If he can show her how to love, they might save each other from the terrors that plague his nights and all of her days.

Available in print and ebook
Like a book? Please consider leaving a review.

ABOUT THE AUTHOR

Jean Davis lives in West Michigan with her musical husband, two nerdy teenagers, and two attention-craving terriers. When not ruining fictional lives from the comfort of her writing chair, she can be found devouring books and sushi, enjoying the offerings of local breweries, weeding her flower garden, or picking up hundreds of sticks while attempting to avoid the abundant snake population that also shares her yard. She writes an array of speculative fiction. Her novels include *A Broken Race, Sahmara, The Last God*. Follow her writing adventures and sign up for her newsletter at
www.jeanddavis.blogspot.com